DEATH BY NUMBERS

A MURDER LEDGER MYSTERY

P. L. HANDLEY

CHAPTER 1

Death was all around. Death was *always* all around.
Johnny Roberts was standing in front of a five-foot gravestone with the name John Llewelyn Roberts chiselled deep into its cold, hard surface. He stared at the three words for at least a minute. Then, he lifted up the rusted handle of his groaning lawnmower and began demolishing an entire row of stinging nettles.

Johnny's middle name was Thomas, but the novelty of seeing his own name on a gravestone had never grown old. Someday, there would be another John Roberts buried in that graveyard and he was doubtful whether anyone would notice.

The Roberts family had buried many people in the grounds of Alwyn's Church. Johnny Roberts was the last in a long line of undertakers and gravediggers, all of whom had bared that same and important legacy. These days, however, the owner of *Roberts Funeral Directors* could not be found measuring up a new coffin or digging another grave. Instead, he had been forced to supplement his dwindling income with a string of odd jobs. Moonlighting as a church groundsman had not been the existence

Johnny Roberts had pictured for himself when he took on his new role.

In a town where the mortality rate was at an all time low, Johnny had begun to doubt whether the business of death and bereavement was such a sensible form of income in the first place.

"If there is one thing I can guarantee you, lad," his father used to say, "there will always be a market for death."

Unfortunately for Johnny, the seaside village of Trebach had since been blessed with the highest life expectancy in the entire country. The population's increased longevity and above-average age range was deemed to be the result of a number of factors: the wholesome sea air, a thriving community spirit, an abundance of health-promoting seafood. The funeral director had yet to fully understand the reasoning, but there was one thing he was quite certain of: the population was going down far slower than he would have liked.

"Have you finished with them brambles yet?" he cried out, after the collision with a large rock caused his lawnmower to die a horrible death.

His younger brother, Rhod, was in his usual position on the other side of the graveyard — perched on a drystone wall and buried in his favourite book. The teenager had never shared his older sibling's hard work ethic, and had the business been left in his own delicate hands, the two brothers would have starved to death a long time ago.

It wasn't that Rhod was lazy or complacent; it was that he just didn't really care enough. Unlike his brother, the young man had never been gifted with the physical attributes required for hours of hard digging, let alone the sheer mental fortitude for not sobbing half way through a funeral procession. Some people were cut out for this line of work and some people were not.

Fortunately for Rhod, *Roberts Funeral Directors* had not received a new client in months.

"Rhod!!"

The younger brother almost fell off the wall, as the roar of his own name sent him stumbling in search of his shears.

Johnny could only shake his head in dismay. It seemed that their business was in big trouble. But, luckily, he had a plan. The man now heading into his late thirties had always considered himself quite resourceful. His entrepreneurial instincts had been dismissed by his father on many occasions. Johnny knew full well that he was worth a lot more than six pounds an hour, and soon he would show everybody.

Although his previous attempts at making it rich had failed miserably (it had turned out that investing in a kennel for fish was not the most sensible business decision), his latest plan was very different. If he executed it well enough, it might even be a way for him to escape that small village at the edge of Anglesey.

The whole idea had started with just a few simple calculations. Funerals were not cheap, and if a new client were to come knocking on Johnny's door, it could easily make them a nice four-figure instalment. Multiply this by at least three clients a month and it could end up being a very good year indeed.

All it was going to take was three deaths per month. But Johnny had a plan for that part as well.

When you'd spent your entire career burying people in large holes, it had become easy to accept death as a very natural part of life. Everybody had their time, and everybody had their reasons. Some people got to far outlive their friends and others were taken much earlier than expected. The way Johnny had come to see it, some individuals lived much longer than they deserved. If some of these people needed a little encouragement in their journey to the afterlife then why not make a handsome profit at the same time?

It was a temporary plan, of course. And there would come a time when it had to stop. But for the coming months, it was time for some of Trebach's overflowing population to pay their dues. Johnny would have to choose carefully, and he would have to remain inconspicuous. He had built up the nerve, and he had a slew of unpaid bills to motivate him. Nobody would know but him.

By the time the funeral director had contemplated his next steps for the third time that morning, the blade of the old lawnmower had fired back into action. Johnny smiled.

Over on the other side of the graveyard, Rhod was wincing from the cut of a stray bramble. He hated having to work during his school holiday. Had his brother not dragged him out of bed that day he would have been pursuing some more important tasks (like watching the new season of *Paranormal Pest Control*). Despite the man's sudden outburst during his small break, Johnny had been unusually quiet that day. It was as if his mind was focused on more than the long grass outside Alwyn's Church. Perhaps it was that pretty new employee over at the hotel, Rhod thought. Or, heaven forbid, there was another doomed business venture on the horizon. Whatever his brother's overactive head was busy concocting that day, the teenager hoped it wasn't anything he had to worry about.

CHAPTER 2

The opening verse of the song "Breathless" by The Corrs did nothing to cheer up Alun's miserable face. If anything, he would have preferred a stone cold silence over a pop tune he hadn't heard since the dawn of the new millennium. Rhiannon had blamed the choice of music on her parent's lean selection of CDs (an excuse he had used himself not that long ago).

"It will be a nice getaway," she had said.

When his driver had first proposed the idea of a long, all-expenses-paid weekend away on the island of Anglesey, Alun had hoped it was going to be the perfect opportunity to take their blossoming new friendship to the next stage. What exactly that stage was, however, he had not yet decided, but he hoped it would at least involve a romantic dinner by the seaside — or maybe even some puffin spotting. Instead, it had turned out that their little excursion beyond the Welsh mainland was purely a "work trip".

Whilst Rhiannon had the privilege of her own en-suite room in a hotel and spa, Alun had been informed that he would be staying in a "delightful" little bed and breakfast down the road.

As far as the accountant was concerned, there was nothing "delightful" about lodging in a stranger's house.

The rooms at the *Balamon Castle Hotel and Spa* were *apparently* in high demand. Built by none other than King Edward I and located just outside the seaside town of Tremor, the historical accommodation was popular among tourists and medieval buffs alike.

After the success of her last article on the mystery of a local witch, Rhiannon's editor was keen for her to follow up her popular story with something equally as "click-bait worthy". The tale of Mary Doyle had resulted in a surge of online traffic to the Merioneth Press website, and with an upcoming documentary and book deal on the horizon, Morgan Morris, the local newspaper head-honcho, wanted to sure that the rights to his top reporter's next assignment remained firmly in his own hands. There would be "no expense spared" he had assured her (except, perhaps, her assistant's sleeping arrangements).

"I'm still not quite sure why you need me to come," said her sulking passenger.

Rhiannon had noticed the man beside her had said very little since they first joined the North Wales Expressway. The major dual carriageway had taken its two travellers along a stunning stretch of coastline, all the way to the narrow Menai Straight. They had later left the great road to cross the world's first major suspension bridge, a structure that still carried its floods of visitors to the most northern county in Wales.

"Oh, cheer up — will you?" Rhiannon begged. "We're entering sunny Anglesey! The accommodation isn't *that* bad."

Alun folded his arms and stared out of the window. He was still recovering from his driver's speedy dash through the bridge's narrow arches. The Victorian crossing had been around for a very long time, and he hoped that the steel cables that lined its enormous edges were not going to choose this particular day to give in.

"It's not just the accommodation," he muttered. "It's... well... never mind."

"If I'd have known I was bringing the Summertime Scrooge with me, I wouldn't have asked," said Rhiannon.

"Then why did you ask?"

She turned to him, smiled and began stroking the top of his head. "Because I need those fresh pair of eyes and that analytic mind of yours."

Alun removed his glasses and wiped away the steam. He wasn't so sure about the fresh pair of eyes.

"For what, exactly?" he asked "You haven't even told me what we're investigating."

Rhiannon was giddy with excitement. She had been looking forward to telling him but thought it was best to wait until he was trapped in a car with no way of escaping.

"We're going to visit a haunted castle," she revealed. "Well, technically it's a hotel now, but that doesn't seem to bother the ghosts."

He should have seen it coming. She had already mentioned the word "ghost" on their telephone call. He had suspected a hint of the paranormal, especially after the success of her recent article on witchcraft, but he had never expected a haunted hotel. Suddenly, the bed and breakfast didn't seem so bad.

"Haunted? Based on what evidence?"

Rhiannon groaned. "I don't know — bumps in the night — a Victorian maid behind the shower curtain — the usual stuff! Why do you always have to ruin all the fun with the need for facts?"

"I'm a man of logic. If something goes bump in the night in my house, it's usually the heating. I don't immediately assume it's my deceased grandmother."

"This is going to be a long trip," Rhiannon muttered, her forehead almost banging itself against the steering wheel. Alun just wished she kept her eyes on the road.

"And what's so special about this haunted hotel?" he enquired again. "Surely North Wales has plenty of haunted locations closer to home than *Anglesey*."

"Ah, well, this is where it gets interesting." Her passenger waited. He hoped she was right. "This particular haunted hotel is currently being visited by a world-renowned paranormal investigator: Don Fletcher."

She waited for the gasp. Instead, her passenger just gave her a blank stare.

"A para — what?"

"A ghost hunter! A whisperer to the undead! A paranormal expert."

Alun was still as lost as ever. The only ghost hunters he'd ever heard of were men in beige jumpsuits who fired out laser beams. It had been a great film, at least.

"How does a person get into a job that involves haunted houses?" he asked.

"You'll have to ask him," said Rhiannon. "Wish our career advisor had recommended that one in school."

Alun pondered over the name. "Don Fletcher... Doesn't sound very Welsh."

"American."

"Ah. Well that makes more sense."

Alun looked up to the rear view mirror to see that the bridge was disappearing behind them, and they were now safely back on land again. The greenery of Anglesey was as vibrant as the green back home, but he could tell he was in a different part of the country now, a different world were the air was salty and the accents were a little stronger. He was homesick already.

"This Don Fletcher reached out to me," Rhiannon said,

failing to hide her smugness. "He said he'd read my article and thought I'd be the perfect person to help him." She saw the frown coming from her left. "That *we* could help him. He said good things about you, too."

Her abrupt attempt to rescue her friend's ego had worked. Alun was rather flattered to be acknowledged by an American ghost catcher (or whatever the man was).

"I'll be honest," she continued. "I didn't have a clue who the bloke was when that first e-mail came through. But after a quick *Google* search it seemed he was worth a reply. Turns out he's working on a new book."

"Fiction or non-fiction?"

She turned to see her passenger's cynical face. "You'd better not start doing this when we meet with him. For the duration of our visit, we will not be referring to ghosts as *fiction*."

Alun sighed. The point was taken.

"So what does Mr Fletcher want us to do?" he asked. "I hope there's not a ouija board involved."

"He said he couldn't go into too much detail until our meeting. But he's been staying at the Balamon Hotel for the last few months — for work purposes. Apparently the place is absolutely riddled. You know, with ghosts and the like. But over the last week he thinks there's something far more disturbing going on."

Alun felt a jitter in the pit of his stomach. It usually happened when the likelihood of danger reared its ugly head. "*Disturbing*?" he asked with a gulp.

"He also used the word *sinister*."

There was another jitter. "Oh, great. Even better."

"Doesn't it sound exciting?" Rhiannon asked. Her body performed a little happy dance in her seat.

"Did he say anything else? Something a little more specific?"

"Just that he'd give an exclusive interview about his new

memoir. He has a big following around the world, so the Chief's happy. Sounds worth it even if we do hit a dead-end with it."

Alun hated her choice of the term *dead-end*. It was bad enough that they were heading to meet a person she had effectively met off the internet, one who had spent most of his life chasing after the deceased. He had nothing more to say on the matter, and they spent the rest of their journey listening to the next instalment in Morwenna Williams' CD collection: *The Lighthouse Family's Greatest Hits*. It was as if the vehicle he was sitting in was a time-travelling Deloreon.

The first stop on their Anglesey leg of the journey was a little seaside village called Tremor. It was not only a ten-minute drive from the hotel and now the location of Alun's temporary residence over the next few days.

Tremor's breathtaking view of the Irish Sea was hard to ignore, even for a grumpy traveller like Alun. The sight of its stone cottages, as they curved down towards the small harbour, reminded him of a model village he played with as a child. Unlike his hometown of Pengower, this was not somewhere you would ever pass through or stumble upon by accident (not unless your map reading skills were truly atrocious). As far as Alun was concerned, he had truly reached the end of the world (and it was a small world at that).

"Oh, look!" Rhiannon cried, as they drove through Tremor's sleepy high street. "There's a fish and chip shop. At least you've got dinner sorted."

Alun let out a grunt. It was easy for her to say. He could only imagine the fine cuisine waiting for her at the Balamon Hotel. His driver then pointed to a small tavern with two elderly men smoking outside. "There's even a pub."

"Great," said the accountant. "That's my Saturday night sorted."

Rhiannon gave him a playful nudge. "Don't you go causing any trouble now, you little party animal!"

Her amusement was not reciprocated. Alun had never cared for the act of sarcasm, but he could smell it a mile off. He was beginning to think that his fellow traveller was finding his situation quite amusing.

"Although, I wouldn't worry too much," she added, looking around at the local inhabitants. "I haven't seen anyone around here under the age of seventy."

Alun peered out of his window at the vast amount of white hair. She wasn't wrong, he thought.

Their car came to a grinding halt outside of a small bungalow.

"Why have we stopped here?" Alun asked.

Rhiannon pointed towards a rickety sign that was barely visible from the main road. Just like the front garden, it had seen better days and featured a description that rocked the accountant to his very core: *Bed & Breakfast*.

The man squinted through his glasses to make sure his eyes weren't deceiving him. "You can't be serious?!"

"Looks cosy," said Rhiannon in her most innocent voice.

"It doesn't even have a star rating!"

"I'm pretty sure it did online."

Alun buried his face in the safety of his palms. "For all we know," he said, "this is just some random person's house."

"A random person called Glenda — at least that's what the reservation confirmation said."

Alun flung out his arms in acknowledgment. "Oh, well, that makes me feel miles better." The use of sarcasm was growing on him.

He climbed out of the vehicle and pulled out his enormous suitcase (the contents was apparently twice the amount of his driver's, but it was good to be prepared).

The bungalow itself was as neglected as the garden, with its pebble-dashed exterior in desperate need of repair. It was hard to ignore the pile of rusted old appliances sitting beside the porch, which had not been moved in quite some time. Alun approached his new accommodation with great trepidation (he presumed the photographs "online" had not been recent).

"Oh, by the way!" Rhiannon called out. "I forgot to mention — check-in time is not until six!"

The accountant turned around to see her frantically winding up the window. "*Six*?! That's another five hours! What am I supposed to do until —"

It was too late. Rhiannon was already waving goodbye. The car sped off, leaving an abandoned Alun to regret his large suitcase. He looked around the small cul-de-sac and could hear nothing but seagulls. It was going to be a long afternoon.

CHAPTER 3

The face of Huw Earnshaw glared on the other side of the glass. It was a cold expression, a look that had haunted many of his former secondary school pupils over the course of his long career.

Johnny Roberts stared right back at him, safe on the other side of the window. He lifted up his wet sponge and slapped it hard against the elderly man's thick double-glazing. The soap sprayed out across the glass and covered up the man's disapproving frown.

"Almost done, Mr Earnshaw!" Johnny cried out.

The funeral director, and part-time window cleaner, let out his most charming smile. He received a scowl in return; it was like detention all over again.

His former teacher let out a short grunt and made the difficult journey back to his armchair.

Johnny began scraping off the excess soap whilst reflecting back on his troublesome school years. He had once been described as a "gifted child", one with a strong aptitude for numbers and arithmetic. Unfortunately, this bubbling potential had later been squashed by the daily reprimands of a certain secondary school maths teacher. Mr Earnshaw had taken a great disliking to him since the very first day, and Johnny had never quite understood why. Perhaps it was the young man's natural disregard for rules and authority.

"The apple has fallen very far from the tree, Roberts!" Mr Earnshaw had always reminded him.

It had turned out that Johnny's father was quite the model student in his youth, and his son was doomed to walk in that shadow until the day of his graduation.

The young funeral director couldn't help but wonder, as he emptied his bucket of brown, dirty water, what might have been his situation had he been offered a little more encouragement. He was quite certain that a few qualifications under his belt wouldn't have hurt, as opposed to the long afternoons he had spent walking the coastal paths of Tremor instead of being in school. If he had spent more time applying himself to homework rather than chasing after girls, then perhaps, he would have found himself somewhere far away from the grimy panes of Mr Earnshaw's front windows.

Still, there was no use wasting any more thoughts on what *should* have been. For Johnny Roberts knew that his fortune was changing. And he also knew, if he applied himself carefully enough, that it would continue with the help of a cranky old man.

"What are you doing in my house?" the retired teacher growled, when he caught sight of his chirpy looking window cleaner standing in the living room.

"Do you mind if I use your toilet, Mr Earnshaw?" Johnny asked.

His question was followed by the obligatory grunt. The old man had been prepared to refuse this unusual request, until he considered the prospect of his worker relieving himself somewhere else on the property.

"Upstairs," he said.

If only Mr Earnshaw had been a man of so few words back in the classroom, Johnny thought. The long, drawling sound of his voice had put many a pupil to sleep over the years.

Johnny approached an old stairlift which seemed to have gathered dust, and he scooted his way to the second floor. It was still strange to see a man who had been such an intimidating figure during his school years become so frail and immobile. He had no problem with the sight of a dead body (and he had seen many over the years), but witnessing the gradual deterioration of a living person was always uncomfortable. It had been hard enough to watch his own father wilt away into a senile version of his old self, a fate that he too would also share when the time came.

Mr Earnshaw's bathroom smelt like the same aftershave that used to hang around in the air of his classroom. Johnny shuddered at the pair of dentures grinning at him beside the sink. He opened up the medicine cabinet and let out a relieved sigh.

The shelves were lined with an array of different pills and medications. His hand rummaged through them, until it landed on the strongest looking painkiller he could find. He swiped away the bottle and thanked his host for such a generous selection. How easy it would have been, he pondered, for such a confused individual to accidentally consume far beyond the recommended dosage. Or, perhaps, it was not an accident at all. He had heard about many who had chosen this method of fast-tracking their journey to the afterlife.

Johnny picked his poison, and with a nervous skip in his step, he scurried downstairs to the privacy of the empty kitchen.

Unlike his medicine cabinet, the contents of Mr Earnshaw's food cupboard was not nearly as well-replenished. It appeared that the old man had managed to live on a diet that consisted primarily of canned sausages and baked beans. Had it not been for the single jar of instant coffee, Johnny would have found his next task quite difficult.

"Fancy a brew, Mr Earnshaw?" he called out.

It was only when Johnny closed the cupboard door that he realised Mr Earnshaw was already stood in the doorway. Those cold, dark eyes gave off a piercing stare.

"What are you doing in my cupboard?" he hissed.

"Uh, well, I was just —" Johnny saw the jar of coffee still in his hand and waved it at him with an innocent smile. "Making us a coffee!"

The pair of eyes studied him with a suspicious squint.

"You were thieving from me!" Mr Earnshaw cried.

"Thieving? Why, no, I was just —"

"Thieving! Like a dirty, little rat! Don't take me for a fool, boy..."

The younger man struggled to reply. It was like he had been shrivelled down to a nervous school boy again. He had been in this exact scenario before, only last time the accusation had come at the disappearance of a confiscated packet of cigarettes. Johnny had always been the usual suspect.

Mr Earnshaw was enjoying the awkward pause. It had been too long since his last tirade of abuse. Human contact was a rarity these days, and the only person he ever met with was his unfortunate care worker. "Once a thief, always a thief!"

Johnny put the jar down. His plan had taken an unfortunate stumble. "Let me make you a coffee."

"I'll tell you what you can do," snapped the retired teacher. He pointed his long cane towards him. "You can help me to the toilet."

His guest was half-relieved and half-apprehensive. He was glad the trial of the food cupboard had come to an end, but he did not like the prospect of helping someone else with their business — especially his rotten, old maths teacher, of all people. He'd already seen what the staff of Plas Madog (the local nursing home where his father now resided) had to deal with.

"This is supposed to be my carer's job," Mr Earnshaw grumbled, as the two men slowly made their way up the stairs, one step at a time. "But of course she's late again. And some things just can't wait."

Johnny let out another heave, as he tried to keep up the enormous amount of weight now hanging around his shoulders. That nurse must have been the size of a wrestler, he thought. His pole bearing duties had been a walk in the park by comparison. At least a dead person didn't try to make it difficult.

"Can't you use the stairlift?" he asked, when they were almost half way up.

"Oh, not that wretched, old thing. I gave up on that the day after they installed it. I don't need a machine to help me up a flight of stairs."

Johnny begged to differ. At least a machine didn't have back problems.

"This is good for you, lad," Mr Earnshaw continued. "A bit of sweat. Your generation don't even know the meaning of it. If you were accustomed to hard work, you wouldn't be cleaning windows for a living."

Suddenly, the weight of the old man had tripled. Johnny could feel his blood pressure rising, and it was a lot quicker than they were moving.

"Can I ask you something, Mr Earnshaw?" he asked, whilst trying to catch his breath. He didn't wait for permission. "Why did you always pick on me all those years ago? Why weren't you as hard on the other kids?"

The old teacher chuckled. "Don't be so pathetic, boy! I only treated people how they deserved to be treated. You were a giant waste of talent — from day one. God had given you a gift, and you squandered it away with laziness and stupidity!"

The words cut deep. They gnawed through the younger man's soul far more than he ever would have realised. Johnny assumed he was referring to his natural ability to process large calculations without the use of a calculator. It had been noticed very early on, but he had never given it much thought back then.

"Do you know how hard I had to work before I earned my degree?" asked Mr Earnshaw. "I had to study twice as much as anyone else just to keep up. And then I have to watch people like you who don't even have to work at it."

Their feet made the final step towards the top of the stairs. Mr Earnshaw's voice had started to fade into a distant echo in Johnny's mind — similar to how it had done during his classroom lectures. He did his best to prevent those harsh words from messing with his emotions. They kept droning on, until the last few sentences came out at full volume.

"You're a waste of space, Johnny Roberts!" Mr Earnshaw roared. "And you always will be!"

Both of them stared at each other. The retired teacher now had his back facing the stairs, and his former pupil was struck by a glimmer of opportunity.

Mr Earnshaw had expected some sort of reaction to his aggressive dose of home truths. In the old days, it would have been in the form of tears. Instead, the man now facing him merely smiled.

Without realising it, at least initially, Johnny had been given a second chance to cement his original plan. He knew that the staircase was steep enough to do all the work, and he knew that a single push was all it would take.

∽

THE BALAMON HOTEL had only been a short drive from the centre of Tremor, but its looming presence and grand exterior was a far cry from the humble cottages of the small village.

Rhiannon stared up at its medieval turrets and ivy-covered walls. The hypnotic mixture of red and stone brickwork was both imposing and beautiful, much like the solid oak doors that had kept out many unwanted visitors over the centuries. This impressive facade was so distracting, the journalist almost knocked over a "stupidly placed" statue in the middle of the driveway. "Fancy putting an ugly thing like that there," she thought to herself, as she swerved around it and tried to ignore its following stare.

The car rolled across the pale gravel and came to a full stop just outside the main entrance. Rhiannon rooted through her handbag in search of a booking confirmation and looked up with a gasp. Lurking on the other side of her window was a pale face with wild hair and shiny skin. The man must have been in his sixties, but his eyes were bursting with the energy of a small boy.

"You can't be here!" he called out, his voice muffled by the thick glass.

Rhiannon wound down her window and was struck by a waft of body odour.

"You can't be here!" he cried again. "You need to go back!"

"What makes you say that?" she asked, her blood curdling from the strange warning.

He drew her attention to the large sign only a few feet away from her bonnet. "Staff parking!"

The journalist breathed out a sigh of relief. "Oh. I see."

"Come!" The man went marching off across the driveway and signalled for her to follow. His fluorescent, yellow jacket gleamed in the afternoon sun, and his posture was hunched over from years of physical labour.

The car followed its guide along a narrow track that led them around the building. They passed through a series of well-maintained gardens that stretched out into the surrounding landscape. The panoramic view was a sudden reminder of quite how isolated this hotel was. Miles of farmland seemed to keep on going, until it reached the sea, which by this point was a faint line across the horizon. The area was a stark contrast to the mountainous region of Rhiannon's hometown.

Having circled around to the back end of the hotel, she parked up next to a cluster of other vehicles. The man in his hi-vis jacket watched with great curiosity, as she unpacked a series of enormous suitcases from the boot of her car.

"I'm fine now," she said, as the presence beside her didn't seem to go away. "Thanks."

"That's a one-point-eight engine," the man said to her, pointing at the car's bonnet.

"Is it, really? How fascinating." She grabbed her luggage and began wheeling it away as fast as possible.

"That's a one-point-four... that one's a one-point-six..." He proceeded to point towards every vehicle in the small car park. After realising that Rhiannon was already halfway across the lawn by the time he had finished, he chased after her.

"Are you some kind of mechanic?" she asked, when the overly friendly stranger came scurrying by her side. Her question made him burst out laughing.

"A mechanic? Me? Oh, no, no, no..."

"You seem to know a lot about cars."

"I don't even drive."

More laughter followed, and Rhiannon would have been quite happy if the man disappeared into a giant sinkhole. She had never been a people-person, especially when it came to the really friendly ones.

When she finally made it back to the large entrance, she was pleased to find that her new friend had stopped abruptly. Like a vampire of the night, it appeared that he was not prepared to go any further than the front door (and this suited Rhiannon just fine).

As the reporter entered the main foyer, she was struck by the overpowering smell of polish and old oak. Daylight poured through from the large bay windows, and it lit up the chequered surface of the tiled floor. The inside of the hotel was a lot more rundown than she had expected. A faded, red carpet snaked its way up an enormous staircase that seemed to dominated the entire room. She looked down at her wheeled suitcase and suspected there would not be a lift.

Over in the corner, in front an enormous painting of King Charles I, was a nervous looking receptionist.

"Can I help you, madam?" she asked.

Rhiannon looked around to make sure no one was following her and whispered: "You might want to do something about that strange man outside."

The young woman smiled. "Oh, you mean, Guto? Don't worry about him. He's one of our volunteers."

"You have volunteers? In a hotel?" The journalist pictured the man's grubby hands. "Not in the kitchen, I hope."

An awkward silence followed.

"Would you like to check-in?" asked the receptionist in her politest of voices (something she had perfected specially for guests she didn't like). She was handed the booking confirmation and began typing the details. "You're on the eastern wing. Room number twenty-three. Breakfast starts at eight. You'll have full access to the spa, pool and gym facilities."

Rhiannon took her room key and, as she thought about a nice massage, had to remind herself that she was not there on holiday. "Actually, I'm meeting a friend of mine at your restaurant. He should be staying here."

"Oh, I'm sorry, we can't give out details of other guests. They're confidential."

The journalist rolled her eyes. She'd heard *that* one before. "His name is Don Fletcher."

The young woman did a poor job of hiding her horror. It was a name she certainly knew, but not one she had expected to hear.

"Excuse me, madam?"

"Does that name ring a bell?" Rhiannon asked, sensing her discomfort.

"Uh, well…" The receptionist cleared her throat. "You really haven't heard?"

"Heard what?"

The discomfort increased, and the woman behind the counter tried to find the words. "Oh, I really don't know what I'm allowed to say, but, well — Mr Pitcher is no longer with us."

"He's left? He told me he was staying for at least another week. Where did he go?"

"I don't think I'm explaining this very well." The flustered receptionist looked around to check they weren't being overheard. She leaned forward and lowered her voice. "I'm so sorry to be the one to tell you this, but, Mr Pitcher has sadly passed away."

CHAPTER 4

The waves of the Irish Sea seemed angry. Alun watched them crash against the rocks and explode into the cold air.

It was supposed to be summer, but the clouded skies had drained the small fishing village of any colour that it might have once had. A handful of tourists were still determined to enjoy their family holiday, forcing themselves to get through a waving bag of cold chips before they were preyed upon by a flock of local seagulls. Alun admired their determination.

He walked back up a long jetty before the tide could beat him to it. After spending the entire afternoon wandering around all of Tremor's narrow roads and paths, the place was slowly growing on him. When it came to a holiday, the thought of a big-city-break filled him with dread, and he much preferred a bit of peace and quiet. He had no need for landmarks or sightseeing tours, and, to his great relief, there were none of those in *this* village. Two of the highlights so far had been a closed sailing museum and a shop that sold primarily wool. What more could a person need?

His mood had altered so much from the dose of salty air that he had even found himself nodding to the occasional passerby. The wheels of his large suitcases continued to rattle away, and he decided to take a quick detour through the middle of a local cemetery. After making a brief acquaintance with the town's deceased residents, he strolled back out into the main street, where he was faced with the sight of a small funeral home.

Before he could check his watch again (for what was probably the umpteenth time that afternoon), he was struck by a small explosion only inches away from his right foot. Looking down, he was surprised to find a splatter of raw egg. He turned to the sky, and when an unidentified flying object came falling towards him, he had the sudden urge to find his umbrella.

"Over there!" cried a distant voice.

Alun turned around to see a teenage boy come running towards him through the graveyard entrance. His clothes were black, and his hair was dyed a shade of fluorescent blue, whilst the long trench coat dangling across his tall, heavy boots almost caused him to stumble as he went. Up in the distance behind him was a horde of rowdy youths, all with grinning faces and a box of chicken eggs in each hand.

They chanted his name out to the theme song of *The Addams Family*: "Duh, nuh-nugh-nugh — Rhod! Rhod! Duh, nuh-nuh-nuh — Rhod! Rhod!"

The teenager named Rhod went charging past a confused Alun, almost knocking him over in the process. Eggs went flying against his back, as his fellow teenagers continued their merciless assault. He sprinted across the road and headed straight for the sanctuary of the closed funeral home.

Alun watched him fleeing his gang of tormentors and couldn't help but feel a degree of pity.

"Oi!" he called out, still conscious of the remaining ammunition in their hands. "Leave the lad alone!"

The teenagers all fell silent. Alun turned around to see that their victim was long gone, and the only person standing before them was himself. He saw the wickedness in their eyes and began to feel a tingle of nervousness (this was, after all, his favourite coat).

Suddenly, the helpless accountant was bombarded with a relentless flurry of projectile eggs. He covered up his face in despair, as the teenagers unloaded everything they had left on him. Egg yolk splattered against his carefully ironed clothes, and he had no choice but to grab his suitcases and flee.

"Chick, chick, chick, chick, chick — en!" came the chants.

Alun wasn't quite sure how a load of people born post the millennium knew the words to a nursery rhyme his own mother used to sing, but he didn't have time to ponder the mystery much further, as he went stumbling away in a desperate bid to find cover.

Just as he was about to give up all hope of rescuing his *Oxblood* shoes, he felt something pulling him towards the funeral home.

"This way!" cried the young voice.

Before he knew it, Alun was being dragged past the window of a long hearse. The teenagers were not too far behind, and it wasn't until they had both slipped through a backdoor that the man and his rescuer could breathe a sigh of relief.

Alun could hear the last of the eggs being pelted against the wall behind him, until the attackers began finishing their chorus of abuse. He wiped some excess yolk from his face and looked over at the teenager huddled beside him.

"Don't worry," he said. "They won't dare come in here."

The teenager with blue hair was not half as rattled as the accountant; it was almost as if he was used to this sort of treatment.

"Why were they chasing you?" Alun asked.

"Why do you think?" came the response. "I don't exactly

blend in round here." He stood up to reveal his gothic clothing and an assortment of jewellery that would make Ozzy Osborne proud. "And neither do you."

Alun agreed that his formal clothes were a little unsuitable for a day at the beach — not that they were still in pristine condition.

"Well, I appreciate the shelter," he said.

"Don't mention it."

The young man offered out a helping hand and lifted him up off the ground.

"How did you get in here?" Alun asked.

"I work here."

Rhod flicked on a series of switches to reveal an entire room full of coffins. Thankfully, they were all empty.

"You couldn't find a paper round?" Alun asked. "That was my part-time job when I was your age."

"My brother runs the place," said Rhod. "Family business, like."

"I know all about *those*."

The accountant peered into one of the caskets and realised it was probably the same size as him.

Rhod could sense his discomfort. "Don't worry," he said. "There's no bodies in here today. Probably why we're so skint."

"I suppose someone has to do it," said Alun, as he could feel the cold draft wafting through the room.

"You get used to it after a while," Rhod assured him. "I used to hate seeing the bodies when I first started, but I don't mind them now. People give you less grief when you're dead."

Alun turned to see the young man wiping some yolk from his enormous boots. He saw the sadness in his face and felt quite sorry for him. "Have you told anyone? You know, about those idiots outside?"

Rhod chuckled. "Tell who? The teacher? Yeah, cause that

always works." He lifted up his large rucksack and checked it for damage. "I don't give a damn what the people of this town think. I'd rather be surrounded by dead people anyday."

Alun looked around again at the coffins. He wasn't sure he quite agreed.

"I've got a gift they'll never understand," Rhod continued.

"Really?" asked Alun. "And what's that?"

The young man stared at him, a surge of excitement bubbling up inside of him. "Do you believe in the afterlife?"

The room fell silent. The accountant had been asked a similar question before, and if he had found it a strange conversation the last time, he now felt like he was stepping straight into the twilight zone.

"Do *you*?" he asked in return, deciding it was best not to answer.

"Of course," said Rhod. "I see them all the time."

Alun gulped. "*See* them?"

"I've been seeing them since I was a boy. They're everywhere."

His guest started slowly making his way towards the door. Alun was starting to see why Rhod had attracted so much attention among his teenage peers. Thinking back to his own school years, it was unwise to go around claiming to see members of the afterlife, especially if you wanted to make friends.

"It's alright. I know you don't believe me. Nobody ever does."

Alun felt the need to avoid the teenager's stare, but he didn't know which way to turn. Suddenly, a bombardment of raw eggs didn't seem so bad.

"No, no! It's not that I don't believe you... It's just..." He tried to think of something to say. "There's not many ghosts round my way. I don't know why. Must be the weather." That disappointed stare was killing him. Then he remembered why had come to Tremor in the first place. "Hey! If you like ghosts, then I hear that hotel down the road is a corker. You'd have a great time there."

Rhod seemed almost amused by the remark. He knew all about the *Balamon Hotel* and its rich history of ghost sightings. "People have always loved to exploit the dead. My family have done that for generations. It's not right, though. Spirits have rights just like we have. That hotel has done nothing to help them. All they do is attract more tourists. It makes me sick."

It had occurred to Alun that his new friend had locked the door behind him on their arrival, and he was now trapped with an apparent ghost activist.

"I couldn't agree more," he said. "Those poor ghosts are just trying to live like we are. Well — not technically *live*, I suppose — especially being dead and all... Haunt, maybe? Would that be the right word?"

"So you *are* a believer?" asked Rhod, leaping up from a coffin he had been sitting in. He lifted up his rucksack and made his way closer to the nervous individual by the door.

"Oh, sure! I used to watch *Casper* all the time when I was younger. I've always loved the friendly ones."

"I knew you were a believer. You seemed like an open-minded person." Rhod reached into his bag and rummaged inside. "I've been working on my communication skills recently. Do you want to see my ouija board?"

Alun thought about it for a moment. The teenager had moved straight into his personal space, and there was nowhere left to move. "You know what? I think I better get going."

∽

THE SUN WAS BEGINNING to set by the time Alun had returned to his small holiday home. He approached the old bungalow with the same trepidation as he had felt the first time. Only *this* time, he was covered from head to toe in a layer of raw egg.

His visit to the undertaker's had ended quite abruptly. As much as he would have loved to spend the rest of the afternoon playing with ouija boards, he had told his budding, young psychic that he was running very late for another engagement and that perhaps another time might have been better.

After finally plucking up the courage to check-in to his new accommodation, he was surprised to discover that his host was already awaiting him in the open doorway.

"Are you my new lodger?" asked the elderly woman with a grin the size of her perm.

"Uh, yes," Alun replied. "I suppose I am."

"What a pleasure it is to meet you, my dear." She walked over to greet him and embraced him in an unexpected hug. "I'm Glenda."

Her guest stood in the middle of the pathway, trapped in a tight squeeze that he thought was going to last forever.

"I hope you don't mind the cwtch," she added. "I've always been more of a hugger than a shaker. Always will be."

Alun felt his body relax from the very moment he was released. "Sorry about the... you know — egg."

Glenda stepped back and removed her thick glasses to take a proper look at him. She was dressed in a flowery cooking apron that clashed with her colourful blouse. Her rosy-cheeked face had an intensity and friendliness that made Alun very nervous. "Oh, my goodness! Look at the state of you. You poor thing!" She grabbed hold of his coat and began pulling him towards the house. "Let's get you settled in so you can clean up. I'll start running you a nice hot bath."

"That's really not necessary," Alun insisted, as he did his best to resist. He felt like running in the opposite direction, as fast as he could. The luggage could be replaced, but his dignity was a little more fragile.

"Now, now," said Glenda. "You're on holiday. And I intend to give you the best one you've ever had. You'll get nothing less than a personable, hands-on service in this house. Not like some of those *other* establishments, who expect their guests to take care of themselves. I've got a fresh pot of cawl on the stove and a TV guide all mapped out for an evening you'll never forget. You can sit in my late husband's old chair. Do you like soaps, Mr Hughes?"

Alun did indeed like a good hand wash, particularly of the *Imperial Leather* variety, but he didn't know why she needed to know that. As the bungalow door slammed shut behind him, he braced himself for an evening as long as his afternoon. The little town of Tremor had made quite the impression on him so far, and he had a sneaking suspicion that there were a lot more surprises to come.

CHAPTER 5

"What do you mean he's *dead*?!"

The news of Don Fletcher's passing had come as quite a shock. Rhiannon's last e-mail from the man had been less than twenty-four hours ago, and as much as the receptionist seemed to be telling the truth, she was quite adamant that there must have been some sort of misunderstanding.

"I'm very sorry, madam," said Gwen. "It happened over a week ago. The funeral's tomorrow."

"*Tomorrow?*"

"I really shouldn't have mentioned it."

"I'm due to have a breakfast meeting with him tomorrow morning!" Rhiannon snapped. "You would rather me wait until then to find out?"

"Uh, no — I just..."

The journalist could see the young woman's flustered mind trying to come up with the right thing to say. She felt a sudden bout of guilt; in her moment of high emotion, Rhiannon had forgotten that the person was just trying to do her job (just like her). Her temper had always been prone to get the better of her.

"I'm sorry," she said. "I didn't mean to be rude. I'm just very confused."

Gwen could see her colleague, Gethin, lurking in the distance. She signalled for him to come over, like a desperate queen of hearts summoning her guards.

"Gethin!" she called.

The man made his reluctant walk across the foyer. His clothes were immaculate, and his gelled-back hair only exposed his snobby frown even more.

Gwen pointed to the luggage. "Help this woman to her room, would you? She's just had quite a nasty shock. It's room twenty-three."

Rhiannon couldn't help but feel as though the woman was merely palming her off and didn't really care for her well-being after all. Gethin was also displeased and grabbed the suitcase as if it were covered in sewage.

"Follow me, madam," he said in a disinterested voice.

The young concierge led his guest up an enormous staircase that circled its way up to the first floor. Rhiannon looked down at the floor beneath them, which now resembled a giant chess board with an absence of pieces. If she had to choose a chess piece that resembled Gethin, it would have been a bishop, with its stiffened posture and pointed head.

"She thinks the sun shines out of her, that one," he muttered to himself, as they entered the first of many hallways.

Rhiannon couldn't help but overhear the comment and could sense his disdain for the young woman. "Happy in your work then?"

"I have no problem with my work. It's the idiots working around me I take issue with."

"I think she was just nervous."

Gethin scoffed. "So would I be if I were her. She only got the job because her auntie runs the place. There's more nepotism round here than the royal family. Doesn't give her any right to boss me around."

The woman behind him turned her attention away from the back of his shiny head and admired the hotel's impressive selection of framed paintings.

"Fifteenth century I take it?" she enquired.

"How the devil should I know?" Gethin asked back. "I'm a concierge — not a tour guide. All I know is that this place was built by some king who had a thing for big castles and drawbridges. Right barrel of laughs from what I hear. How's that for your history lesson?"

Rhiannon caught a brief glimpse of the king in question, who was staring at her from one of the passing works of art. "Good enough for me. I've never been one for castles, personally. Not unless there's a siege."

A faint smile pushed its way through her guide's mouth, like a splinter that refused to budge. He was starting to like this woman. "Don't get me started on all those lords and ladies who came afterwards."

Considering the building's impressive legacy, Rhiannon couldn't help but notice its deteriorated state. Its poor upkeep was clear, and she was starting to question the cost of her booking. Fortunately, she wasn't the one paying.

"This place could definitely do with some tender love and care," she said. "Who owns it nowadays?"

Gethin scoffed. "Someone who's as old and decrepit as these walls. She also happens to be the manager's widowed mother, Angela Pugh. What are the odds of that?"

Doors flickered past them, as the concierge quickened his pace. Although the hotel was practically falling apart, it was still a far cry from the journalist's usual accommodation at the edge of a busy motorway. She had seen more travelodges than a seven-tonne lorry, and none of them had come close to the vast scale of the Balamon.

"If you hate working here so much, why don't you leave?" Rhiannon asked.

"Oh, I'll be leaving soon enough. Don't worry about that. My talents are wasted around here."

"And what talents are those?" She looked down at the perfect seams along his trousers. They were as straight and narrow as the man's spinal column. "Ironing?"

Gethin stopped for a moment and turned around. "Opera, actually."

"*Opera?*" Rhiannon had not expected that one. "Never had you down as a singer."

"Never had you down as such a nosey parker."

"Well, I'm afraid being nosey is an occupational habit. It's why I'm here in the first place."

"You're not a copper, are you? We've had plenty of those around recently."

"Really? And why's that?"

The young man wanted to smile but thought it was probably a little inappropriate.

"It's not everyday we find a dead guest," he said. "Shame it doesn't happen more often, actually. It would make my life a lot easier."

"I presume this guest was Don Fletcher?" Rhiannon asked, as they passed into yet another long hallway. She was beginning to wonder whether she would ever find her way back. Surely they had crossed into the East Wing by now, she thought.

"Don Fletcher..." Gethin shuddered. "Now there's a name I never thought I'd hear again." He stopped abruptly outside one of the doors and pulled out a key. "Here we are."

Rhiannon was as relieved as the concierge. It had been a

long way to lug such a heavy suitcase, and she had let him take the heavy one.

They entered the large room, which did not seem to have been updated since the seventies. As nice as it was to have a four poster bed to herself, she dreaded to think of the amount of people who might have slept in it.

"Your en suite, madam," Gethin announced, still trying to sound professional despite the obvious lack of interest. "The telly should work and I'm told the bedding is clean."

Rhiannon was drawn to the large window lighting up the entire room. It overlooked the main gardens and reminded her of a Renoir painting.

The concierge headed back towards the door and was halted by another question.

"Something tells me you weren't really a Don Fletcher fan?"

"Paranormal investigations?" scoffed the man. "I think the old man was potty." He thought about him some more. "*And* rude. There were times when I could have throttled the man."

He caught Rhiannon's glare at the unfortunate choice of words.

"And did you?"

"Of course not. Luckily for me, he took the liberty of taking care of that part himself."

"So it *was* a suicide..."

The concierge began checking the cleanliness of the room with the help of his natural dirt radar. He had always possessed an obsession for tidiness, whether it was his own sleeping quarters or anyone else's. The dust on the windowsill had been obvious from the moment he had walked in.

"Hardly surprising the man killed himself," he muttered. "I heard he had a morphine habit. They found him lying in a full bath, apparently. Dosed up to the eyeballs."

"So it was an overdose?" Rhiannon asked. She was still

baffled by the man's complete lack of sympathy. He must have been as cold as the room temperature.

Gethin turned to look at her. "What does it matter? The man's dead. And good riddance. He was the worst guest we've ever had."

"That man's a good friend of mine, actually," she lied. Don Fletcher had been more of a recent pen pal, but she couldn't wait to see the shock on the concierge's face. She was not disappointed.

"Oh, well I — uh," he stammered, before quickly trying to change the subject. "Would you look at that!" He pointed to the empty pillow. "She's forgotten the spare towel and complimentary chocolate. I'll bet you this was Mared's room. Stupid girl. Should have done the job myself."

Without a moment's hesitation, the concierge had scurried to the door quicker than a flustered parrot.

"Enjoy your stay, madam!"

Rhiannon did her best to hold in the laugh, but it soon found its way out once the door had slammed shut. Serves him right, she thought to herself. The fact he was a snitch only made it even more satisfying.

She looked around the room, and as comfy as the bed looked, it did nothing to absorb the feeling of loneliness. There she was — all the privacy in the world — and all she wanted was someone to share it with. If the *Balamon Hotel* was haunted, at least she would have some company.

It had not been easy leaving her three-year-old son, Gwyl, in the hands of her overbearing parents. An evening of babysitting was one thing, but an entire long weekend was proving to be too long a stretch.

What if he began loving them more than her? What if they brainwashed him? What if they couldn't remember the bedtime routine?

This string of paranoid questions was making her doubt whether the trip had been worth it at all. Now that she had heard about Don Fletchers' untimely demise, she knew for certain that it hadn't been.

A few hours later, she was lying on the bed with a 'share size' bag of crisps on her lap and her phone resting against one ear.

"Why is he not in bed yet?" she asked.

Her mother's high-pitched drawl could be heard screeching out from the end of the receiver: "You do know I've raised a child before?"

Rhiannon wanted to point out that her bedtimes were the strictest known to man, but if she wanted an over-tired three-year-old on her hands, then so be it.

"You know, his eating habits have really gone downhill since you both moved out," her mother continued. "He won't even touch sweetcorn now."

"That's because he's probably not hungry enough. How many snacks have you given him?"

"Oh, I see. It's all *my* fault now, is it? You can't just starve them all day."

Her daughter could hear the crunching noise, as she squeezed the bag of crisps in her hand as hard as she could. The conversation was making her realise how desperate she had become for company to endure such torture.

By the time the call had ended, she was a furious ball of energy. Perhaps that hotel spa would come in handy.

The glow of a summer sunset could be seen pouring through her enormous window. Silence had descended on the hotel, and it was driving Rhiannon mad. It was worse than her new home in the quiet little town of Pengower.

When realising that the batteries in her television remote control were flat, she turned her attention back to the mobile phone. There was *someone* out there she could speak to. It was a person she could always depend on at any hour of the day.

"How you getting on?" she asked, after dialling a name that, with thanks to his first initial, appeared very high in her contact list.

"Is that supposed to be funny?" asked Alun's voice. "I'm sitting in an elderly woman's living room, watching my third soap opera of the evening."

Rhiannon tried not to laugh. "Careful, or she'll hear you."

"She's feeding the cat. Did you know I was allergic to cat hair, by the way? Glenda has five of them."

This time the chuckle slipped out, and there was a long pause on the other end of the line.

"At least you've got someone looking after you," said Rhiannon, lying back against her large pillow and stretching out her body with all of the free space.

"I don't need looking after," Alun said. "I just need some privacy for five minutes."

"Well, it's not too much better over here." She wrapped herself in the feather duvet.

"If you say so."

The sound of a famous soap theme filled Rhiannon's ears. Even without seeing her friend's face, she knew he was cringing.

"Hey!" she said. "You'll never guess what's happened." The reporter looked over at her door and kept her voice down. "Our friend Don Fletcher's only gone and carked it."

Another long silence followed.

"He's dead?" asked Alun.

"Killed himself, apparently. They found him overdosed in a bath of water."

"Are you telling me this whole trip has been a complete waste of time?"

"Well, here's the thing — I've still got my meeting tomorrow morning."

"With Don Fletcher? I think he's unlikely to turn up for that one, isn't he? Especially considering he's not alive anymore."

Rhiannon rolled her eyes. She knew he must have been in a bad mood. He was always sarcastic when he was grumpy.

"I'm quite aware of that part, thanks," she said. "What I mean is that Don has been dead for a whole week. Those e-mails I received when setting up the meeting came through afterwards. Which means one of two things: either the ghost of Don Fletcher has hijacked his e-mail account, or —"

"Someone else has been pretending to be him..."

"Bingo!"

"But why? And *who*?"

Alun could hear the cogs of his friend's brain whirling around and could picture the twinkle in her eye.

"There's only one way to find out," Rhiannon said. "See if they show up for the meeting."

"You really think they will?"

She shrugged. "Either way I get breakfast. Fancy joining?"

CHAPTER 6

Rhiannon gasped. She opened her eyes to see her pillow was drenched in a layer of sweat. Streams of daylight poked through the edges of her curtains, and, from the melodies of birdsong, she knew it must have been morning.

She normally had no trouble sleeping, but her first night at the *Balamon Hotel* had been one of continuous tossing and turning. The nightmare she had just experienced featured some of the most vivid imagery she could ever recall: howling faces, never ending hallways, a flaming building. Stanley Kubrick would have been proud.

Had it been the binge of late-night junk food? The overdose of horror films during her youth? Or, was the hotel indeed haunted, after all?

Before she could give it any further thought, Rhiannon was showered and dressed in record-breaking time (it was amazing how quick a person could get ready without a three-year-old).

When it came time to open up her room door, she was met with a presence more startling than the monsters in her dream. Standing in the middle of the hallway was an elderly woman with a piercing stare. She locked eyes on the disturbed guest and remained frozen like a curious snowman.

"Mrs Pugh!" a voice called out from the other end of the narrow corridor. "I haven't forgotten about you!"

A young cleaner called Mared came running over and began escorting the woman back up the hallway.

Rhiannon bolted for the stairs before anything else could jump out and startle her.

Downstairs, she passed through the main lobby and followed her nose towards the hotel restaurant. She entered the small dining hall to find only two occupied tables: an elderly couple enjoying their breakfast and a reclusive looking teenager in the far corner. Although she was pleased not to be the only guest in this large hotel (she had seen few so far), there was certainly a feeling of disappointment. The journalist had at least hoped to come across the perpetrator of her mysterious e-mails, as unlikely as that may have been.

The room was much loftier than your average hotel dining room and had clearly boasted a few banquets in its time. All that remained now was an impressive ceiling with a disused chandelier dangling above a small arrangement of tables.

Rhiannon was just about to help herself to the meagre buffet of food, when she noticed someone approaching her from behind.

"You must be Rhiannon," said the person in a floral dress as loud as her voice. The woman's earrings were large enough to be a health and safety hazard, and they swung from side to side in time with her curling hair extensions.

"How do you know my name?" the journalist asked in a baffled voice.

"I saw it on the booking." She offered out a handful of bright purple fingernails. "I'm Liz Pugh — the manager here at the Balamon."

Rhiannon relaxed her body and accepted yet another blow of disappointment.

"I'm so sorry for your loss," said Liz. "I hear you were a friend of Mr Fletcher's."

"Where did you hear that, if you don't mind me asking?"

"Oh, there's not much that gets past me in this hotel, I can assure you of that."

The hotel manager let out a proud grin and almost forgot herself for a moment. There was something about the woman that disturbed the hungry journalist. She knew a sociopath when she saw one.

"It's such a shame about Mr Pitcher..."

"It's Fletcher," Rhiannon corrected.

"He was one of the loveliest guests we ever had. He'll be truly missed around here."

"Is that right?"

Her cynical guest couldn't help but remember the concierge's opinion from the day before.

"He was with us for months, you know," Liz continued. "This place was becoming a second home to him. And we'd become his newfound family."

Rhiannon forced out her own giant smile to the point that her cheeks hurt. "Well, I can't blame him. It's such a... *lovely* hotel you have here. Strange it's so quiet for this time of year?"

Her words had landed with the desired effect, and the manager's face was now reeling underneath her thick layer of makeup.

"Yes, well... It's been a little slow this season, but there's still plenty of time for things to pick up." Liz straightened out her dress and stood tall, as if she was an army drill sergeant preparing for a march. "Now if you will excuse me. Please do enjoy your breakfast."

Rhiannon watched her enormous heels go trotting off, until

she was free to plate up her food. She sat herself down in the far corner and kept a close eye out for any new diners.

After tucking into her dry bread, she noticed a shadow covering her table. Towering above was the teenager she had seen upon entering the room, and he was now standing opposite her with a nervous grin.

"It's you, isn't it?" he asked.

The journalist looked up at him with a confused frown. He was wearing thick glasses and his hair was an unnatural shade of blue.

"Do I know you?" Rhiannon asked.

"Uh, well, yes — sort of." He looked around the room and gave an awkward shuffle. "I don't mean to interrupt your breakfast, but —"

"Are you going to sit down, or what?" Rhiannon hated being interrupted when there was food to be eaten. But she hated awkward individuals who refused to get to the point even more.

The young man, known as Rhod, pulled out a chair and joined her at the table.

"Sorry for having to meet like this," he said. "It was the only way."

The woman opposite squinted at him. "Meeting? What meeting?"

Rhod pushed up his glasses, which had a habit of sliding down at the most inconvenient of moments. "Well, yeah. The e-mails, remember? We arranged to meet here."

Rhiannon dropped her knife. It clanged against her plate like a penny dropping into a steel bowl. "Wait, you mean — Don Fletcher's e-mails — that was *you*?"

The teenage became sheepish, although he also seemed proud. "I'm a big fan by the way. Ever since I read your article on that witch — I just knew you'd be the perfect person to help."

Flattery had done nothing. The confused journalist was still baffled and annoyed. She hadn't come all the way to Anglesey to meet with some fanboy who had impersonated a deceased medium.

"Sorry I'm late!"

They both looked up to see an out-of-breath Alun taking off his coat. The accountant sat himself down and got his first proper look at Rhiannon's dining partner. His jaw dropped.

"It's — *you*!" he cried.

The teenager with blue hair grinned. "*You're* the accountant? The one from the article? I had no idea!"

Alun and Rhiannnon looked at each other.

Rhod was clearly overwhelmed. He had read the newspaper article at least a dozen times since its publication and could never have imagined he was going to meet both of its main heroes. The fact that the whole story had taken place in North Wales was exciting enough.

"So how do *you two* know each other?" Rhiannon asked, pointing at the people who had managed to gatecrash her breakfast.

"Uh, we sort of bumped into each other," said Alun, trying to forget that lingering odour of rotten egg.

The journalist shook her head. She didn't want to know. "I can't believe I've been so stupid."

"So how do you two know each other?" Alun asked.

"We met online," said Rhod.

"No, we didn't!" Rhiannon snapped. "This man here is an imposter. I should have you reported to the police."

The teenager glanced around the room. He wished it wasn't so quiet. "No — please! I didn't mean to upset you, I just — it was the only way you'd ever meet with me."

"So you thought you'd pose as a man who's just taken his own life? What are you — sick and deranged?"

Rod could feel the beads of sweat pouring down his acne-prone forehead. Sweating had always been an issue at times of stress, and times of stress seemed to be a regular occurrence in his life.

"What makes you so sure he took his own life?" he asked.

His question had succeeded in grabbing their full attention.

"What makes you think he *didn't*?" Rhiannon asked back, sensing the teenager's confidence. It was the type of confidence a person always had when they knew more than the people around them.

"I got to know Mr Fletcher quite well over the course of his stay," said Rhod. "He still had plenty to live for. Like finishing his new book."

Rhiannon peered into his glasses and almost caught sight of her own reflection. "They say he overdosed. People who overdose don't always intend to kill themselves, but they do if they're lying in a bath full of water."

Rhod shook his head. "Mr Fletcher was very specific with his doses. He'd been doing it for years."

"How does a teenager like you end up hanging out with a man old enough to be your grandad, anyway?"

Rhod almost appeared irritated. "He wasn't just *any* man. He's the most famous medium who ever lived."

"The most famous medium who ever died, you mean," Rhiannon corrected. "A bit ironic if you ask me."

"When I first found out he was coming to Tremor, I couldn't believe it," the young man said, his eyes wild with excitement as he recalled hearing the news. "I'd read all of his books and teachings. My brother was already doing odd shifts here at the hotel, and I asked if I could help. That's when I got to meet Don."

"Lucky you," said Rhiannon. "I hear he was quite volatile."

"He might have been a little... *eccentric*, at times. But the man had a gift. It's not an easy one to bear. I know that myself."

Alun sat there, listening. He remembered the young man's enthusiasm for ghosts during their first encounter and was not in the least bit surprised at what was being said. The arrival of Don Fletcher must have been like Tom Jones rocking up at Pengower Town Hall.

"I started helping him with his séances," Rhod continued. "It was a dream come true. He taught me so much."

Rhiannon could think of better company for the night than a person who sought out the dead, but she let the young man enjoy his moment.

"Did he ever seem depressed or keen to end it all?" she asked.

"Quite the opposite. He seemed... scared. Well, at least, he did towards the end."

"Scared of what?"

Rhod could feel his heart racing. "He mentioned dark forces. Like something in the hotel was trying to kill him."

"Like a person?"

"More like a spirit. An evil one."

Alun shuddered. He was already getting flashbacks of his time discussing dark magic with Mary Doyle. His world of logic and reason was being flipped on its head, once again.

Rhiannon let out a deep sigh. "If you've got us all the way over here to conduct an exorcism, then I'm afraid you're barking up the wrong tree. You might not realise this, but I'm actually a proper journalist." She ignored the raised eyebrow coming from the direction of the accountant. "I like to uncover the truth — not some mystical creature who lurks in hotel corridors."

"But in your e-mail you said the idea of a haunted hotel was perfect for your next story."

Rhod's comment had stumped her. "Yes, well... that was before I knew I was dealing with some random teenager from Anglesey. At least Don Fletcher had some serious ghost credentials. I was hoping the article could be more about him than the ghosts themselves."

"It still could be," said Alun. The other two turned to him, surprised by his sudden interest. Whilst they had been discussing the likelihood of evil spirits, he had been going over the facts. "What if Don Fletcher *has* been murdered? I don't know about dark forces, but it sounds like his death is rather suspicious. He sounded adamant someone was trying to kill him. What if that person was human?"

Rhiannon was listening, but not yet convinced. She leaned across the table to look the teenager in the eye. "Did you tell the police about your last conversation with Don?"

Rhod shook his head. "They didn't seem very interested in Don's work. I don't think they really believed in any of it. I did tell them about his drug habit, though. They seemed a lot more interested in that."

"I bet they were," said Rhiannon.

Alun's mind was alive with curiosity. It had been a while since it had a new puzzle to sink its teeth into, and it was keen to get working on a new one (even if there was in fact no puzzle to be solved). "Did anyone else know about the drug habit?"

The teenager gazed up towards the enormous ceiling with its elaborate decoration and grand design. He pondered the accountant's question for a moment before attempting his response: "I think all the staff probably knew. He was quite open about it. Said he used it to mask his mood swings. Apparently one of the cleaners used to get him a fresh supply every once in a while. He said she used to tip her really well."

"All we need now is a motive and we might be onto something," Alun said, leaning forward in his chair. He could feel the juices flowing and couldn't wait to get to the bottom of it all. Rhiannon, on the other hand, was not nearly as enthusiastic.

"Well that shouldn't be too hard," she muttered. "The

concierge hated the old man with a passion. I can't imagine any of the other staff members liking him." Another sigh escaped her lips. "I don't know... It could all be a massive waste of time if you ask me."

She rose to her feet and surprised her two companions with the need for an abrupt exit.

"Where are you going?" asked Alun.

The journalist turned around with a shrug. "What any sane person would do in a hotel and spa — I'm going for a quick swim and a massage. You coming, or what?"

The accountant contemplated the idea of having his muscles man-handled like a piece of doe and couldn't think of anything worse. But the swim sounded okay.

"Well, I suppose a quick dip couldn't hurt."

The journalist, the accountant and their budding, young medium headed out through the Balamon's main doors. A morning mist had gathered outside, and the surrounding gardens possessed an almost magical quality.

"I suppose there's worse places to be stuck in," Rhiannon said, breathing in the fresh air.

Over on the other side of the gravel driveway was a man mowing the lawn. She admired his dashing good looks and muscular frame. Alun couldn't help but be repulsed by the woman's wolf whistle.

"Glad to see not all the volunteers around here look like the *Hunchback of Notredamn*," she said, taking in the view.

Rhod felt like jumping behind the nearest rose bush. "He's not a volunteer."

"A professional gardener?" Rhiannon admired the muscular frame. "Even better. I love a man with green fingers."

She watched the man look up to notice them standing there on the stone steps. He pointed to the teenager in the middle and cried out: "Rhod!! Get here — now!"

Rhod gave a sheepish glance before he scurried off towards him. "Got to go," he said to them. "That's my brother."

The journalist watched him run off, as Johnny Roberts gave her a quick wink.

"That's his *brother*?" She turned to Alun, who didn't see the appeal at all. "I suppose we could always stay here a few more days. You never know what we might uncover."

The accountant had been oblivious to her seductive tone, until the sudden change of tune made him very suspicious. He turned to see that she had already walked off towards the spa and took another look at the strapping young gardener with his solid frame and full head of hair. He still couldn't work out what all the fuss was about.

CHAPTER 7

Johnny Roberts reached out and grabbed his packet of cigarettes from the bedside table. Sitting himself up against the headboard, he lit up and enjoyed a long, hard drag of smoke. He had always wondered why people always tended to smoke after making love. Now he knew why. It wasn't just to look cool in one of those black and white detective films. Instead, it had turned out that the surge of nicotine was a perfect accompaniment to the rush of endorphins that had overcome him only moments before.

After gazing around the room at the luxurious surroundings, he turned his attention to the woman who was frantically getting dressed.

"What's the matter?" he asked her, studying the receptionist's frazzled movements.

Gwen hadn't even noticed he was watching and was keen to get the room back to looking exactly as they had found it. Perhaps choosing the most prestigious room in the hotel hadn't been a good idea after all.

"We need to get out of here or someone will see us," she said, buttoning up her blouse as fast as her shaking fingers would allow.

"No, I mean in general," said Johnny. "You seemed really off today. Tense, even."

"It's nothing," she replied and scooted over to the window to peer outside. "I don't think we should be doing this."

She saw the undertaker putting out his cigarette in the glass beside the bed and wanted to choke him. Gwen marched over and snatched the glass away. "Not another thing to clean!"

Johnny grabbed her by the arm and pulled her towards him.

"We're doing no harm," he said. "We're both young, both single. Why don't you tell me what's really the matter?" His attempt to seduce her back into bed failed miserably.

"I told you — it's nothing!" the receptionist shouted and yanked her arm away.

The room fell silent.

Gwen froze and was shocked by her own outburst. She sat herself down on the bed beside him and allowed the distress to consume her.

Johnny watched her with his calm and collected face. He was rarely startled and waited for the woman to speak again.

"I'm sorry," she said, eventually. "It's just — I've had another letter..."

Those cold and calculated eyes of the man beside her flashed. He *knew* there had been something wrong. Johnny hadn't been seeing the receptionist for very long, but she was very bad at hiding her emotions — unlike him.

"What letter?"

Gwen tried to pull herself together and grabbed hold of the handbag that was lying on the floor. She pulled out a slip of paper and showed it to him. The letter had clearly been typed out on a computer and featured a single sentence: *If you value your life — leave here and never come back!*

"You've had *another* one like this?" Johnny asked.

Gwen nodded. "The first one was slipped under my door the day Don Fletcher died."

Ah, yes, Johnny thought. The American who killed himself; he had heard all about *him*. Don's passing was going to be a nice addition to his growing billing list (the second booking that week). News had already come through about the passing of his former maths teacher, and he had offered his sympathies to the family. Still, one family's loss was another person's gain.

"If I didn't know any better," said Johnny, "I'd say that was a good-old-fashioned death threat." His words had offered the woman little comfort. "What did the first one say?"

Gwen fought to hold back the tears. "It said: You are not welcome. Danger waits for you at the Balamon."

The man nodded. "Well, at least that one was more specific."

The young woman fell into his arms, and he felt her sobbing against his chest. After tapping her on the back a few times (despite his profession, consoling people was not his forte), he reached for his pack of cigarettes and offered her one. She declined.

"Any ideas on who it could be?" Johnny asked.

Gwen looked up into his inquisitive eyes and decided to shake her head. Secretly, she knew *exactly* who had written the letters but was determined to keep that little fact to herself for the time being.

"I'm sure they're just empty threats," the undertaker added. "I wouldn't let them upset you. How long until you start your shift?"

The receptionist checked her watch. "Another couple of hours."

Johnny held her in close. "Go take it easy. Find a way to relax for a while. A dip would do you good. Who doesn't feel better after a quick soak in the pool?"

∼

"Argh!" Alun cried. "It's freezing cold!"

His toe had barely touched the water, before he knew that the swim had been a very bad idea.

Rhiannon couldn't help but giggle at the sight of this grown man in oversized swimming shorts, cowering at the edge of the swimming pool.

"Just jump!" she cried out.

The accountant shrivelled up like a soggy leaf and wished he could hide away his puffy torso. Going shirtless had always made him self-conscious, and now he had an audience who was observing his every move from the other side of the pool.

Alun did his best to make a confident leap into the water but, instead, managed to fall sideways with a loud *yelp*.

The journalist giggled and continued with her lengths. She hadn't been on holiday for a very long time, but this little trip to the coast was starting to feel quite enjoyable. As always, this feeling of relaxation didn't last long, and her mind soon began to ponder the strange circumstances of Don Fletcher's death.

"Do you really think he killed himself?" she eventually asked, as Alun came bobbing towards her like a lost buoy.

"Rhod doesn't seem to think so," he said with a mouthful of water.

"The police don't seem to have deemed it suspicious. So there can't have been a struggle."

"I'm no expert on drugs, but I don't think anyone would struggle with a load of morphine inside of them."

Alun ran through the scenario in his mind. Even if they knew who the killer was, it would be very difficult to prove.

"So it all comes down to motives and timings," he said.

"Maybe the killer-ghost theory is more likely, after all," said Rhiannon with a sigh.

She lay back until she was floating in the water with the ease of an inflatable lilo. Just as her body began to fully relax, she heard a piercing scream.

Alun and Rhiannon both looked at each other with the same, horrified expression. Water went splashing in all directions, as they frantically hurried out of the pool. Once they were back on dry land, the two of them charged in the direction of the hotel gym.

They passed through a myriad of exercising equipment, until a banging noise led them to the sauna room. Alun gasped at the sight of an entire dumbbell rack positioned in front of the sauna door. A frantic voice cried for help from the inside, whilst puffs of steam poured out from the narrow gap in the blocked door.

"You take one end, I'll take the other," Rhiannon said, grabbing her side of the heavy obstacle.

Alun took his own position on the other side, and they groaned with all of their might until the pile of weights were dragged out of the way.

The sauna door came flying open, and a flustered and very hot young woman came charging out. She collapsed to her knees and began gasping for air, her skin a bright shade of red.

"What on *earth*?!" Rhiannon cried, recognising the person as Gwen, the hotel receptionist.

"Let me get you some water," said Alun, who rushed off for the nearest water tank.

"I need to get out of here!" Gwen cried. She was very much in shock, and had started to resemble a partly-cooked lobster.

Rhiannon saw the fear in her eyes and held her tight. "Come with me," she said.

Moments later, all three of them had relocated to the safety of the journalist's hotel room.

Gwen was now fully clothed and sitting on the bed. Still traumatised by the near fatal experience, she huddled up into a tiny ball and tried to stop herself from shaking.

"I was just lying there with a towel on my face," she said. "I heard a loud splash of water, and by the time I sat up, whoever had come in had closed the door again. They must have poured a whole bucket onto those heating rocks, because the temperature was unbearable."

Her two rescuers hung on her every word.

"Why do you think someone did this to you?" Rhiannon asked.

"They're trying to scare me away." Gwen's expression turned from upset to angry. "But I won't let them think I'm afraid. They won't win."

Alun chose his words carefully. "Why would someone want to... *scare* you?"

The receptionist didn't have to think for very long about the answer. "Because I know what this person did."

A chill had entered the room and it turned her listeners cold.

"And what's that?" Rhiannon asked. She could hear Alun's gulp, who was already apprehensive about the answer.

"I know they killed Don Fletcher."

CHAPTER 8

"Are you really telling us that Don Fletcher was *murdered*?"

Rhiannon's question seemed to hang in the air for a moment, whilst the shaken receptionist began to regret her previous statement.

"I don't have any proof," she said. "But I saw someone leaving his room on the night he was found dead."

The journalist turned to look at her friend before making her inevitable follow-up question. "And who was it?"

"I can't say."

"You can't remember, or you don't want to?"

"Neither."

Alun decided it was time to include a question of his own.

"Did you tell the police about this?" he asked her.

"I couldn't." After realising what she had just said, Gwen turned to him with pleading eyes. "And *you* can't either."

The accountant shook his head in disapproval. "We can't tell them about something we didn't see for ourselves. I think that's *your* responsibility."

Now it was time for Rhiannon to intervene. She took the

young woman by the hands and knelt down in front of her. "It's okay," she said. "We're not going to tell the police anything. What makes you think that the person who's been harassing you is the same person who you saw leaving Don's room?"

Gwen closed her eyes and reflected back to the moment in the hallway.

"Because I know they saw me," she insisted. "I was coming down the stairs leading to the third floor. We were both as surprised as each other. I could see from the clock in the hallway that it was just about to turn eight. Don usually had a hot chocolate sent to his room for this time, and he was found dead five minutes later by the person who delivered it."

"So the person leaving the room would have known he was dead?" asked Rhiannon.

"Maybe they didn't," said Alun.

"Oh, they knew," said Gwen, the redness in her face having faded into a shade of white. "I saw the look in that person's eyes. They were soaking wet and covered in foam. They also had a pile of pages under their arm." She shook away the disturbing image and turned to her two listeners. "You can't tell any of this to *anyone*."

Rhiannon was still knelt at her feet. "We won't tell the police. You have my word."

Alun paced back and forth in front of the window. "This is quite serious, Gwen. You could be a key witness in a murder. You need to tell the police."

Gwen avoided his eye contact, focusing her attention on the carpet instead.

"I can't," she said.

"Why not?" asked Alun.

"Because I wasn't supposed to be there!"

Her emotional outburst startled the rest of the room.

"I've said enough," said the receptionist, leaping to her feet and grabbing her bag. "I need to get out of this place."

Rhiannon watched her scurry towards the door and chased after her. "Gwen — wait!" She placed her foot against the bottom of the door to prevent it from opening. "Can you answer me just one thing? You don't have to tell me who you saw. And I won't tell any of this to the police. But was the person you saw... was it someone who works at this hotel?"

Gwen stared back at her. She could see the seriousness in the reporter's face and took a leap of faith. The receptionist nodded. After receiving the confirmation she wanted, Rhiannon removed her foot.

The door slammed shut, leaving the other two to fully contemplate what they had just heard. Now that they were alone, Alun decided to make the first appropriate comment: "Have you *completely* lost your mind?"

"What do you mean?" Rhiannon asked, collapsing down against the enormous bed.

"You promised her we wouldn't tell the police."

"And we won't."

Alun looked around the room and tried to keep his voice down. "We're talking about a possible *murder* here, Rhiannon!"

Rhiannon didn't seem anywhere near as concerned and laid her head back against the pillow. "Right now, we're talking about a suicide. That's all anyone knows. One eyewitness account won't be enough to convict a murder anyway, and it will just put Gwen in more danger."

Alun's legs went weak, and he also now felt like a lie down. "I can't believe I'm hearing this. You're talking about withholding valuable evidence."

"We're not *withholding* anything. If Gwen doesn't want to tell the police what she saw, we can't make her. But we can help to put the rest of the pieces together."

"*Pieces?*"

"We already knew something suspicious was going on. It's why that strange teenager brought us here in the first place. Now we're just one step closer to finding out what really happened."

The accountant peered out through the window. The absence of mountains only made him even more gloomy than he already was. He caught sight of a blue coastline stretching out across the horizon and was reminded of where he was. "And why does it have to be up to us?"

"Because I'm a journalist. And I hate getting only half a story."

"Let me rephrase my question." Alun turned around and prodded his own chest. "Why should I get involved in this?"

Rhiannon smiled. "Because you know as well as I do that you can't bear to leave a puzzle unsolved. And you've just come across one doozy of a puzzle, Alun Hughes." She could feel his furious gaze and decided to sit herself up so that they were face to face.

"Alright," she said, "how about this — we spend the next few days getting as much info as we can. Then, anything we *do* find, we'll hand it straight over to the police."

Her friend contemplated the proposal with great suspicion.

"*Everything?*"

"Everything."

Alun's silence had been enough. Rhiannon jumped to her feet and patted him on the back.

"Great! Time to get our hats on Watson!"

She grabbed her coat and began putting on her shoes. Her sidekick remained quiet until she was fully dressed and ready to unlock the door.

"Anywhere in particular you want to start?" she asked.

"Yes," said Alun. The journalist turned around to see that he was still standing there in a pair of baggy swimming shorts and a towel. "Can I at least find my clothes first?"

∼

THE COFFIN of Don Fletcher was lowered into the empty grave. Johnny Roberts watched another body enter the earth as he had done countless times before.

This particular burial had been a rather unexpected addition to his growing client list. The young funeral director had been expecting only the one funeral that week and had now been blessed with a second. Unlike Mr Earnshaw's booking, this one had required no preparation whatsoever. If only it was always so easy, Johnny thought to himself.

The presence of a famous American psychic had been common knowledge among the locals of the town, but only one of these people had been familiar with the name. Dressed in his formal work attire, Rhod Roberts lost all sense of professionalism, as he watched his hero and friend disappear into the darkness. He normally felt nothing during a routine ceremony, but, this time, he was overcome with emotion.

"Stand up straight," his older brother whispered to him. Johnny was making a poor attempt to appear dignified, and the teenager's relationship with the old man had always struck him as unhealthy. He would never understand the desire to befriend a person old enough to be his grandfather, especially one as eccentric and strange. But there were a lot of things about his brother he would never understand.

Moving his attention to the small congregation standing nearby, he saw that it consisted of almost the entire *Balamon Hotel* staff roster. Management had insisted on paying for the funeral (a gesture clearly triggered by the awkwardness of having a dead guest in one of their rooms). Johnny had been more than happy to accept payment and had offered his part-time employer little sign of a discount. Business was business.

Once the last handfuls of dirt were dropped against the hard shell of Don's new resting place, the small group of mourners wasted no time in making a swift exit back to their cars.

"Popular man, then," Johnny muttered, turning to his brother. To his great surprise, Rhod had disappeared from his side and was now standing alone in front of the quiet grave. The older sibling shook his head in bewilderment and left the last remaining member of the congregation to his own thoughts.

As Johnny made his way back to the hearse, he caught the eye of a young woman loitering near the entrance. He ignored the lanky man beside her, and they exchanged a flirtatious smile.

Rhiannon took one last look at the handsome, young funeral director and headed inside the graveyard.

Rhod was still standing opposite Don's grave, when two people appeared either side of him. It was only once he had recognised their faces that he turned to acknowledge them.

"What are you both doing here?" he asked.

"Just paying our respects," Alun answered.

"And we really need another chat," Rhiannon added.

In the space of twenty minutes, all three of them were sat round a table at Tremor's favourite local pub: *Y Gafr Wen*.

Alun looked around the empty bar. Plates of finger food were all laid out with nobody to eat them.

"Where is everyone?" Rhod asked. "All the mourners were told to come here afterwards so we can celebrate Don's life."

The pair opposite him both looked at each other. It was clear the teenager was very upset by the poor turnout.

"Well, that's exactly what we'll do," said Alun, raising up his pint glass. "Let's have a toast — to Don Fletcher!"

His gesture seemed to be very much appreciated, and they all clinked their drinks together.

"To Don Fletcher!"

Sips were taken and a long silence followed. The sound of Fleetwood Mac's "Seven Wonders" filled the void for a couple of minutes, until Rhiannon decided it was time to begin their discussion.

"It was a good turnout from the hotel staff," she remarked, a comment that seemed to annoy the teenager more than its intended purpose of cheering him up.

"They're just showing their faces," said Rhod. "The manager made it mandatory for everyone to attend."

"Did she now?" Rhiannon was not surprised in many ways. Some companies would do anything to save face.

"They even paid for the funeral."

Absolutely *anything* to save face, the reporter thought.

"That was nice of them," she said. "A person might even think that they felt guilty about something."

Rhod looked up from his drink for the first time since they had sat down.

Rhiannon tried not to smile. "We spoke to Gwen, the hotel receptionist, yesterday. She seems to think something very untoward happened the night of Don's death. A little bit like you."

"I don't just *think*," said Rhod. "I *know* he didn't kill himself."

"The coroner can't have found anything suspicious," said Alun. "The funeral seems to have gone ahead without much delay."

"So there was clearly no struggle," Rhiannon added.

"But then, there wouldn't be with an extra large dose of morphine inside of you."

"Is there a chance Don overdid his dosage that night?"

Rhod shook his head. "Don always kept his dosages the same. He used to tell me that he'd worked out the perfect amount to keep him steady. I never liked his drug habit, but he never listened when I asked him to give it up. He said it was far better than nicotine or alcohol."

"And what made him start on the morphine in the first place?" Rhiannon asked.

"He had a bad back injury from when he fell off a horse. The morphine was the only way he could feel normal. But he still drank and smoked all day. He didn't like people judging his bad habits."

Alun looked around again at the empty pub. "Judging by the small turnout for his funeral, he obviously didn't have much in the way of family or friends."

"Hardly any," said Rhod. "I asked about his family once and he said he'd moved halfway across the world to escape them. He also said friends are for the weak-minded."

"He sounds delightful," Rhiannon muttered.

"You said *moved*," Alun said. "But he was travelling, wasn't he? He hadn't moved here."

"Don was looking for a house here."

"In Anglesey?" Rhiannon asked.

Rhod nodded. "He told me his ancestors had all come from this island and that he wanted to come home. He'd sold off all of his belongings in Colorado, including his house."

"So he was technically homeless?" asked Alun.

Rhiannon raised an eyebrow at him. "If you can describe an en-suite hotel room homeless. It's hardly sleeping rough."

"He had a lot of money saved up and decided to stay at the hotel for as long as he could," Rhod continued. "Don reckoned the Balamon was once in his ancestor's possession. He showed me a huge family tree that he'd put together. It dated back as far as Cromwell. He even had a theory that he was a descendant of Owain Glyndwr."

"The *last prince*?" asked Alun, brimming with excitement. A painting of the famous Welsh figure had featured on his bedroom wall as a child, and it was a history he had grown very familiar with.

Rhiannon was keen to return to a more recent history and attempted to steer their conversation back to the present: "Didn't you mention in an e-mail that Don had arrived at the Balamon towards the beginning of the year?" Rhod nodded. "Are you telling me that the man spent six months living in a hotel?"

A second nod almost knocked the journalist off her stool. She could barely stand a few nights in a hotel room and struggled to imagine spending half a year in one.

"That's quite the bill he was racking up," said Alun, forever weary of the financial implications.

"He even paid the hotel extra," said Rhod.

"No wonder he was throwing his weight around," said Rhiannon with a scoff. "He probably felt like he owned the place."

"I suppose he did rub a few people up the wrong way." Rhod thought back to the countless incidents involving verbally abused staff. "But I guess that's just what happens when you're a bit different to everyone else. All geniuses can be a bit eccentric. Don was one-of-a-kind. He had a gift that couldn't be wasted. He was willing to spend as much time as he needed to finish off his research."

"Research?" Rhiannon asked with a tone of cynicism. She had heard enough of this idol-worshipping (even if the repast she was attending was for the idol in question).

Alun let out an awkward cough. "I think the research he's referring to is about the — you know..." He didn't want to say the word out loud and hoped she had got the message.

Rhiannon eventually took the hint. "Oh, right! Yeah... the haunted castle thingy."

The accountant couldn't help but cringe. Fortunately, Rhod

was used to people not taking him seriously and didn't appear to be offended. In fact, he seemed quite excited.

"So, does this mean you're staying to investigate?" he asked. "I'll help in any way I can." The teenager saw that the journalist had her notebook open. "You can refer to me as Rhod if you like — for the article, I mean."

Rhiannon saw him gazing at her notes and chucked her pen down. "Where were you around the time of eight o'clock on the night of the eighteenth — the morning Don died."

Alun was more shocked than the teenager. The woman's direct approach had, as per usual, caught him completely off guard. Her eyes squinted like narrow apertures, scanning her interviewee's every move for a hint of dishonesty.

Rhod became overcome with nerves. He hated an interrogation and had been subjected to enough of those at home. "Uh, I was at home."

"Doing what?"

"I was watching the new *Doctor Who* special."

"Can someone else vouch for that?" Rhiannon asked.

"Uh, no — I mean — yes! My brother was home too. At least, I *heard* him come home. Then I found him sleeping on the sofa later on after I heard the shouting."

"*Shouting?*"

Rhod began to look even more uncomfortable than he already was. "My brother, he — he has these violent dreams... He recently had to take all the objects off his bedside table after he smashed a lamp."

Alun couldn't bear to listen any longer. "It's alright, Rhod." He leaned across the table and placed a hand on his shoulder. "We're just trying to establish where everyone was located. That way we can get a clear picture of timings. I'm afraid my friend here can be a little... *aggressive* with her questioning."

Rhiannon felt a nudge against her leg. "Alright, we'll leave it there for now." She leaned forward until her nose was almost touching the young man's quivering face. "But I've got plenty more questions."

Rhod breathed a sigh of relief, as his two companions stood up and stepped away.

"Was that really necessary?" Alun asked, the moment they were out of earshot. "The lad's just buried his only friend and you're grilling him like a prime suspect."

"*Everyone's* a prime suspect in a case like this," Rhiannon hissed. "Even little Pugsley over there. We question everyone the same way. We're here to find out the truth."

"Well maybe I should do the questioning next time."

"What's the matter with my questions?"

Just as she was about to jump down Alun's throat, she noticed they had been joined by a third wheel.

"So what's our next move?" asked Rhod, rubbing his hands together, as the other two stood either side of him. "Do we check the scene of the crime? Or how about drawing a map of the hotel? Yeah, a map! This is way more exciting than I ever thought it would be!"

A furious Rhiannon turned to look at Alun. All he could do was shrug.

CHAPTER 9

T*he scene of the crime.* If there was ever a good place to visit during an unofficial murder investigation, it was the exact spot where the victim had drawn their last breath. Rhiannon had watched more than enough Inspector Morse episodes in her lifetime to know that.

"You know, I could get sacked for doing this," Gethin remarked, as he led the way through the dingy hallways of the second floor.

"Do you really care?" Rhiannon asked.

The grumpy concierge thought it through for a moment. "No, not really."

The concierge had also been quite happy to accept the forty pounds he had just been slipped. It wasn't like the guests staying at the *Balamon Hotel* ever tipped, and as the journalist was willing to pay him over triple his hourly rate for a quick ten-minute peek, it had been the easiest forty pounds he had ever made. Had she thrown in another tenner, he would have been quite willing to dance around on the bed.

"Can I just point out that this is also highly illegal," said Alun, trailing behind them. "This is technically a break-in."

"Nothing you haven't done before," Rhiannon reminded him.

Her comment shut the man up for the remaining duration of their walk. He couldn't argue with *that* point, however, he also wanted to point out that it hadn't been his idea last time.

The concierge reached that all too familiar door at the end of the hallway and pulled out the key.

"Are we sure the manager isn't around?" Alun asked. He looked back again to make sure they hadn't been followed.

Gethin turned to Rhiannon. "Is he always like this?" Rhiannon nodded. "*Always.*"

"Don't worry," said the concierge. "Liz has gone into town for the afternoon. She won't be back for hours."

He opened up the door and revealed a room that had been frozen in time since the departure of its last guest. Clothes were scattered across the floor among a sea of cardboard boxes and piles of dusty boxes.

"Talk about making yourself at home," said Rhiannon, as she tripped over an old kettle.

"So Don really *had* moved in," said Alun, who was in awe at the random selection of possessions the man had managed to cram inside such a small space. Items such as an old analog radio and a broken vase were of particular note. As a man of order and routine, the accountant could never understand how a person could live in such chaos.

Gethin switched on a light, which only highlighted the abundance of clutter even more. "Hardly anything's been moved since the police were here. Liz said she's waiting for the probate to go through before she shifts it all."

"You mean she's the executor?" asked Rhiannon.

"The what?" asked Gethin, trying not to put his hand on any of the grime.

"The person responsible for carrying out the will," Alun explained. "It's normally a trusted family member."

Gethin scoffed. "Didn't sound like that crusty, old man had much in the way of family and friends. If he did, I'd pity the lot of them." The concierge looked over to the door to make sure it was closed. When he discovered that it indeed was, he turned back to the other two with a mischievous grin. "You know he's only gone and left everything to the hotel? How sad is *that*?"

This tiny nugget of gossip piqued his listeners' interest.

"How do you know that?" Rhiannon asked.

"He used to tell everybody. He flaunted that will of his around like a police badge. Acted like he owned the place, he did. Treated us staff like trespassers in his own house. He spoke to us all like dirt — except for Liz, of course. He loved sucking up to her."

"The hotel manager?" asked Alun. "Any ideas on why he would be so friendly with her?"

"Why do you think?" the concierge asked back. "Her mother owns the place."

A silence followed, whilst the new revelation began to take hold.

"Isn't that the old woman who lives upstairs?" Rhiannon asked, trying not to picture the pale face that had startled her only a few hours ago. "I saw her this morning."

Gethin pulled out his tobacco and began rolling a fresh cigarette. He was well overdue for his sixth break of the day. "Madder than a hatter that one," he said. "She's like the walking dead in this place. Gives me the creeps." His long fingers were flickering away at the rolling paper, until they had produced the perfect cylinder to continue his smoking habit. "Not surprised someone robbed her."

Alun and Rhiannon were in the middle of their inspections,

when they both paused what they were doing and turned to face him.

Gethin slipped the cigarette behind his ear and noticed their surprise. "You not heard about the robbery?" He let out a wicked smile. "I need to stop being such a gossip."

Rhiannon had disliked the concierge from the moment they had first met. She knew his type and had worked with a few. There was always one person in a workforce that enjoyed causing trouble, and Gethin was no exception. If stirring the pot was a hobby, the concierge had made it a full time job. Some people lived to upset the apple cart.

"When was this robbery?" Alun asked.

Gethin raised an eyebrow. "I was expecting you to ask *what* was stolen. Isn't that far more interesting?"

"It depends on when it happened."

Rhiannon was as confused by her friend's question as the concierge, but unlike him, she had grown used to strange questions.

But her patience was wearing thin. She knew the young man was enjoying his little game, and if there was anything she hated more than cryptic questions, it was playing games.

"Alright, *what* was stolen, then?"

"No idea." He waited for the groan. "But rumour has it, the old bat lost something priceless."

The concierge seemed very pleased with himself. Clearly he was a very bored man, Rhiannon thought.

"*When* was she robbed?" Alun asked again.

The concierge decided to give in. "It was reported on the eighteenth."

"The day after Don Fletcher died?" Rhiannon asked. She had never been a whizz with numbers, but she didn't need her accountant's help with that conclusion.

"Interesting," Alun muttered, who didn't seem half as surprised.

"Well, that's a huge coincidence, isn't it? Two crimes in one day?"

Rhiannon's second sentence passed through the room like a gust of wind. The concierge stared at her, his mind ticking away on its never-ending timer.

"*Two* crimes?" he asked.

The journalist felt the glare of her furious friend, as she realised the carelessness of her big mouth. Instead of indulging the curious staff member with an answer, she decided to change the subject.

"Was there anyone who Don Fletcher got along with in this hotel?" she asked. "Apart from the manager?"

A disappointed Gethin sighed and turned his mind to the pool of hotel staff (most of which he loathed just as much as the guests).

"I suppose that brother of Johnny Roberts seemed to like him," he said. "Which shows just how strange that young man is."

"We're familiar with Rhod," Rhiannon said. She was just glad they had managed to shake him off back at the village. She had not shared Alun's opinion that he might have been useful. Three was most certainly a crowd when it came to investigating a murder.

"Anyone else?" she asked.

The concierge grumbled at the thought of one individual in particular. "There's a cleaner who used to run errands for him. She'd fetch him his precious prescriptions. But that was just a convenient business arrangement."

"The morphine?" Rhiannon lifted up her notepad and was ready to take a name.

"She thinks nobody knew about her little drug dealing. But

there's not much that gets past me around here. I know what she was up to — that smug, little Mared Tudor."

The name was scribbled down in messy handwriting. Rhiannon had always been thankful for computers, or she would have been the only person in the world to have read her writing.

"Do you know who found the body?" Alun asked, turning back to look at the bathroom.

Gethin looked at him with growing suspicion. "You ask more questions than the coppers. You some kind of detective?"

"He's an accountant," Rhiannon called out, as she routed through a pile of books.

"Oh," said Gethin, almost a little disappointed. "Say no more." He followed Alun into the next room. "He was found by Carys, the assistant manager. She was bringing up his evening hot chocolate. Then she found the suicide letter on his desk."

They stood over the empty bath where Don Fletcher had inhaled his last breath. Unlike the room next door, the environment was void of any belongings and had a fragrance of artificial lavender and eucalyptus. Had the bathroom not been the location of a recent death, Alun would have been quite happy to make full use of the amendments.

"Did anyone else see his body?" he asked, trying not to picture a lifeless corpse floating in the soapy water.

"A couple of people on duty rushed in after they heard the scream," said Gethin.

"Scream?"

"Carys' scream." The concierge snarled at the thought of his assistant manager. "She can be a bit of a drama queen. Gets flustered at the best of times. She runs around this place like a crazy chicken sometimes." He let out a sly grin. "Mark, the chef, does a good impression."

"But you never saw the body yourself?" asked Alun, turning

to the most unlikeable young man he had come across in a very long time.

Gethin shrugged with a sigh. "Afraid not. Shame really. I would have quite liked to see that miserable, old git after he'd kicked the bucket. Wouldn't have looked so smug and self-important then, would he?"

Alun tried to take his remark with a pinch of salt. He knew the man was trying to shock him for his own amusement. At least, he hoped that's what he was doing.

When the two men walked back into the bedroom, Rhiannon was still foraging through the cardboard boxes.

"Find what you're looking for?" the concierge asked.

"Who said I was looking for anything?" the journalist asked, making it very clear she had found nothing.

Gethin looked at his watch. "If you're not careful, this is going to cost you an extra twenty."

Rhiannon climbed to her feet and marched up to him. His smarmy grin was wiped away by the presence of her furious face, only inches away from his own.

"You don't see many of these around," said Alun, pointing to the old typewriter in the middle of the desk. His effort to break the tension had worked, and the uncomfortable standoff had been abandoned for the time being. Rhiannon joined him for a closer inspection of this unusual word processor that was taking up so much room.

"Don't get me started on that ugly, old thing," Gethin muttered. "A poor member of staff almost broke their back getting hold of that for him. The guy hated computers, apparently."

Alun looked around for any signs of typed paper. "This must be what he was using to type out the autobiography he was working on," he said. "There's no sign of any manuscript."

"Looks like it wasn't his first book," said Rhiannon, who lifted up an old paperback.

All three of them gathered around to look at the faded cover consisting of a young Don Fletcher in his prime. Dressed in a long overcoat with an enormous collar, his steely expression gave the journalist a shudder.

"He clearly thought a lot of himself," she said. "Definitely not my cup of tea."

A more curious Alun took the book from her and scanned the title: *Chasing Spirits*.

"Do you mind if I hold on to this one?" he asked.

"Be my guest," said the concierge.

"Whatever floats your boat," agreed Rhiannon.

After she had decided that the additional twenty-pound note was not going to be worth their while, they all headed back out into the dingy hallway. Opposite the doorway was a staircase leading up towards the third floor.

"How many rooms are up there?" asked Alun.

The concierge finished locking up the room behind them and snorted his way to a response: "That's *Her Ladyship*'s quarters. Hardly anyone's allowed up there."

"As in, Angela Pugh?" Rhiannon asked, trying to ignore that pale face again, lurking at the back of her mind. "The owner of this hotel?"

"You can call her what you want," said Gethin. "She won't be able to hear you."

Alun stared at those carpeted steps with their red surface burning in the rays of sunlight. "So whoever stole from her would have probably used those stairs."

"Unless they're Spider-Man. The only other way off that floor is through a window. And I wouldn't fancy my chances heading out of one of those."

The accountant nodded with an intrigued face that made Rhiannon want to slap him.

"Now if you both don't mind," said Gethin. "I've got a much needed ciggy break."

The slender man with his overly-polished shoes marched off to top-up his nicotine levels.

"Lovely man," Rhiannon muttered. "It's amazing this hotel is still making money with *his* level of customer service."

Alun was still fixated on the staircase. "What makes you think that it is?"

She turned to look at him. "Is — what? The customer service? Or the money?"

"The money."

"Trust you to be thinking about the finances."

The accountant shrugged. "Well, look at the place — it's practically falling apart. And they're hardly fully booked."

"Who cares? You're not their bookkeeper."

"Where there's money, there's a motive." Alun looked down at the book in his hand, as well as the intense stare of a young Don Fletcher. "Shame I can't stay the night with all these vacant rooms."

Rhiannon grinned. "You've got a lovely bungalow to get back to," she said. "That woman will be wondering where you are if you're not careful."

Alun grimaced. He had been trying to forget. After seeing the amused expression on his friend's face, the accountant was glad that the Balamon was haunted. Perhaps the spirits that supposedly walked these corridors were also into keeping their guests awake at night. He thought again about Glenda's home-made soup waiting for him back at the village. He would have preferred to take his chances with the ghosts.

CHAPTER 10

It was nearing dinner time by the time Rhod had made his way through the front door. He was used to finding his own meals and was surprised to find his brother already home.

"Where have you been?" Johnny asked, as he was found buried in a pile of company paperwork at the kitchen table.

"I went for a walk to the lighthouse," said Rhod. He hated being questioned, even when there was nothing to hide. He would have liked to ask where Johnny was most of his time but knew it would come with an earful.

"Should have known it was somewhere strange. I saw you talking to those people from the hotel again."

"You did?" Rhod was slightly taken aback by his brother's natural surveillance skills. It seemed nowhere was safe from his watchful eyes.

"Who's the woman?" asked Johnny, with a mischievous twinkle in his eye.

The teenager ignored his gnawing stare and headed for the cupboards. "Just a journalist."

"A journalist?" The undertaker grew even more intrigued. "What did a journalist want with the likes of you?"

Rhod opened up the fridge and was disappointed by its bareness. Jam on toast again, he decided. "She's writing an article about Don."

"The old psychic?" Johnny's curiosity had been dashed. "Seems like they'll cover anything these days."

His brother wanted to point out that Don Fletcher had been more than just a psychic, but he couldn't be bothered to argue.

"Have we got any jam?" he asked.

Johnny leapt to his feet and clapped his hands. "We'll be eating a lot better than jam, lad!" He lifted up a sheet of paper. "You see this? Another job! Just came in this morning."

Rhod tried not to groan. "What are we doing this time? Selling ice cream?"

The older man's good mood was to be short-lived. "What did you just say?" He stormed over and held him in close. His brother cowered at the feeling of a large hand against the back of his neck. "Do you know how much I do to keep your lazy little backside afloat? We'd be sleeping with the seagulls if it weren't for me!"

Johnny could feel him shaking and became satisfied with the reminder of who was in charge. Rhod was soon released and his brother's tone had returned to a more jovial approach.

"This, here," said Johnny, "is another funeral booking! We've had more in the last few months than we had the whole of last year. We're making a killing!"

The young undertaker couldn't help but chuckle at his accidental pun. He waved the document in the air and did a little jig around the table.

Disgusted by the man's extreme moodswing, Rhod made sure to keep his distance.

"Who died?" he asked, pretending to care.

Johnny opened up the shopping bag sitting on the counter and cracked open a beer. "Do you remember Mr Earnshaw?"

"The old maths teacher?" Rhod did remember. Fortunately the man had retired by the time he had started secondary school, but the teacher's fierce reputation was the stuff of legend among those old enough to remember.

"Turned out he fell down the stairs," said Johnny. "Who'd have thought he would go out that way, eh?"

The man slurped the excess froth from his drink and turned his mind to the pretty stranger that had been occupying his brain all afternoon. "Hey, you know that woman you've been talking to..."

The blood running through Rhod's veins went shooting up towards his head. He could see the inner workings of his brother's decrepit mind firing away and knew what was about to be asked.

"You think you could introduce me to her?" asked Johnny.

"Why would you want me to do that?" Rhod asked in return, as he tried his best to act naive.

The undertaker came creeping over like a hungry predator. "Oh, I don't know... Maybe we might get along. Who knows — it could be the start of a beautiful friendship."

His brother could smell the beer, as he chuckled at him within close proximity. Johnny waited for the response, and when he could see that he was failing to get one, he became irritable. "So what do you reckon?"

Rhod could feel the heat of his body on him again like a returning rash. He tried to answer but could only speak in short mumbles.

"*Well?!*"

"I don't know, Johnny," said the teenager. "She's here on business, and, well... she's working with me."

He waited for the wrath of a fire breathing dragon but felt it was worth the abuse on this occasion. To his great surprise, his brother didn't even bite his head off. Instead, the man chuckled again, until it morphed into a howling laugh.

"Hold on a minute!" Johnny cried out. The man allowed the teenager his personal space again but continued his humiliating stare. "You don't think —" Another burst of laughter followed. "That's priceless! Little Rhoddy Roberts thinks he's in with a chance of bagging some woman from out of town?"

"No, I never said that."

Rhod's words did nothing to de-escalate the tirade of mockery that was about to follow. The sound of another beer can opening made him wince.

"You really think a *woman* — of any kind for that matter — would be interested in a weedy, little hermit like you?" The young man could see the hurt he was inflicting and basked in every second of it. "God bless you for trying, lad! Maybe there's more man in there than I gave you credit for."

The teenager wanted to curl up into a small hole, especially when that large hand began ruffling his hair and slapping him on the back.

"We'll call you — Romeo Rhod!" Johnny cried.

As the man began dancing around the kitchen like a medieval jester, his brother had decided he'd had more than enough ridicule for one evening. Johnny had barely noticed him leave the room, and when he approached the front door to reach for his coat, something caught his eye in one of the recycling containers.

Nestled in the used paper box was a crumpled invoice with a familiar name. Beneath the words *window cleaning* was the customer reference *Earnshaw*. Rhod stared at it for a moment before slipping the document into his pocket.

GLENDA PRICE WAS STANDING in her front doorway when Alun returned to his holiday home. How she could sense his arrival, even before he had opened the garden gate, he would never know.

"There he is!" said Glenda. Her cat, Harry, was also there to greet him and was purring in her arms like a Bond villain's pet. "I was beginning to worry about you, lad."

She gave her guest the obligatory squeeze and escorted him inside with an excitement that only seemed to invoke more suspicion.

Alun entered his room as if it were a gruesome crime scene, and he found the entire contents of his suitcase all laid out across the bed. His clothes had been neatly arranged into piles, and it was the sight of his folded underwear that was the greatest cause for concern.

"All your washing is done," said Glenda, beaming with pride beside him. "Sorry about the hole in one of the shirts. My iron isn't what it used to be." Blissfully unaware of her lodger's horrified expression, she closed the curtains and turned on his bedside lamp. "Now — would you prefer your first snack with Emmerdale or Corrie?"

It wasn't long before Alun was back on the streets of Tremor. He wandered, aimlessly, like a lost puppy in search of his next meal. His attempt at a last-minute reason to leave the house had somehow worked, but he knew the well of excuses would soon run dry.

The local fish and chip shop provided at least a brief moment of solace, and with the sun beginning to set, for yet another day on the isle of Anglesey, he decided that a walk along the waterfront would be the perfect accompaniment to his dinner in peace.

Unlike the previous day, the sea was calm, and its stillness gave off an eerie tone that carried over to shore. If it were to be the calm before the storm, then at least it looked pretty.

Fighting off the seagulls in a desperate attempt to keep his piece of cod to himself, Alun saw someone in a long, dark trench coat sitting amongst the pebbles of the small beach. He was clearly no holiday maker, and his black clothes almost camouflaged him into the grey stone. Had it not been for his blue hair, he might have disappeared altogether.

"You dropped your fish," the young man said to him as he approached.

Alun turned around to see his piece of cod being torn apart by a pair of winged scavengers. Perhaps the lad was indeed psychic after all, he thought.

"I prefer haddock, anyway," he said and sat himself down beside him.

Rhod was quite pleased to be offered up a tray of chips and grabbed himself a handful as if they were precious gemstones.

"Shouldn't you be at home?" the accountant asked, scooping up his own mouthful of deep-fried indulgence.

The teenager stared out to sea and was reminded of why he had chosen to spend his evening among the seagulls.

"I'd rather be washed away right now," he said.

Alun had taken the hint and recognised the aftermath of a domestic argument when he saw one. "Fair enough. Say no more."

The unlikely pair of loiterers sat in silence, whilst they both munched on the remaining chips.

"It was a good burial today," Alun said, eventually. He hoped that his gloomy companion didn't mind talking shop, but he assumed that this was the sort of conversation that funeral directors normally had.

"My brother would agree with you," said Rhod.

Alun presumed he was referring to the tall, dark and surprisingly handsome young undertaker that he had seen in the graveyard.

"Your father must be very proud," he said, before catching Rhod's confused glance. "You know — having both of his sons running the family business, I mean."

"My brother, Johnny, runs the business," Rhod corrected. "And my father's in a nursing home, waiting for him to fail."

"Oh. I'm sorry to hear that."

"My brother wouldn't be. He'd do anything to prove our father wrong — anything to keep the business going. But if you ask me, he's just wasting his time. Da' will never treat us the way mam did." A glimmer of hope flashed in Rhod's eyes, like the glow coming from the nearby lighthouse floating in the water. "I still speak to her sometimes."

"Your mother?" Alun asked.

"She was the first person who made me realise my gift." Rhod looked at him with a curious stare. "They stay with us, you know. The people we lose."

"Oh, I'm sure they do."

The accountant tried to hide his cynicism, but he knew the teenager had seen straight through it. It wasn't the first time a person had questioned the word of a self-proclaimed mingler of the dead.

"I see you carry a person," Rhod added, looking around his shoulder as if a third presence was hovering in their midst.

"Excuse me?" Alun asked.

"A man... Someone you lost too early?"

Alun checked over his own shoulder again, but as far as he was aware, there was nobody standing there.

"I did lose my father a couple of years ago," he said.

Rhod nodded. "That makes a lot of sense."

"Are you telling me you can *see* him?"

"Every now and then I catch a glimpse. It's a lot harder in broad daylight. Spirits tend to be more visible at night."

How convenient, Alun thought. Although he would be lying if he admitted that he wasn't just a little bit curious. He would have given anything for one last conversation with his father.

"He seems to want to reassure you of something."

His words created a thick lump in his listener's throat. "Like what?"

"It's hard to tell. I'd need a proper reading."

Alun sighed. He was determined not to be lured into the strange realms of this young man's world. He caught sight of a lump of bait dangling down from a nearby fisherman's hook and decided he would not be that curious fish.

"I picked up my latest bedtime read today," he said in an effort to change the subject.

Rhod looked over at the old paperback in the man's hand and glared at the cover. Another ghost had just presented itself in the form of a young Don Fletcher. The image depicted a confident psychic in his prime. His blonde hair was a stark contrast to the dark clothing, and his eyes were wide with an intensity that had remained until his last months.

"That's a first edition print," said Rhod. "Where did you find it?"

The book title, *Chasing Spirits*, glared at him in the evening sunlight.

"My journalist friend picked up a copy from his room," said Alun.

"She took it?"

Alun sighed. It pained him to admit it. "Yes, she's good at doing things like that. I'm sure she plans to return it when we're finished."

The teenager was handed the book, and he took it as if the man was handing him an old relic.

"Although," Alun continued. "There's only so much you can learn about a person from a book."

Rhod nodded. He understood exactly. He had learnt far more about his hero during his stay at the Balamon than he had ever done from reading his books.

"When they told me it was suicide," he said. "I almost believed it at first. It made me feel like I could have done something to prevent it. What if he had just changed his mind at the last minute? He could have just reached down and pulled out the plug. One yank and he would still be here."

"But you don't think it was a suicide, do you?" Alun asked.

The teenager shook his head. "Are you telling me that you're going to help me find out who killed Don?"

"Quite the opposite." Alun readjusted his position against the rocks. They made for a very uncomfortable seat. "We need *your* help."

His last sentence lifted the young man up from his gloomy mood. He waited with great anticipation for Alun to elaborate.

"We do indeed have reason to believe that *someone*, other than the man himself, took the life of Don Fletcher that night — someone in that very hotel. For all we know at this stage, the murderer could be alive or they could be dead. Either way, I'm sure you can probably help us seek out the truth."

Rhod nodded. He had been on board long before it had been made official.

"You know more about that hotel than we do," said Alun, climbing to his feet. He was too sore to stay seated. "So, how about it? Will you help us?"

The young man didn't even need to reply. His answer was clear.

They shook hands, and for a split second, Alun could have sworn there was a third person beside him.

CHAPTER 11

Rhiannon squirmed as she felt two large hands making their way around her neck. A pair of long, muscular forearms began to clench and tighten, until she wanted to scream out in pain.

"Just relax..." said the voice.

She took a deep breath and tried to resist her natural urge to fight back. With the clicking sounds of her upper back, she felt a release of tension that seemed to have been trapped for quite some time.

The Australian man towering above her possessed a radiant complexion, one that a pasty reporter like her could only dream of. His chiselled features and rugged good looks had been an added bonus to the massage, and Rhiannon had decided that her impromptu visit to the hotel spa had been exactly what she had needed.

"I don't know what you just did," she said, "but it was better than..."

The trainer, known simply as Billy, peered down at her with his playful, blue eyes. "Better than what?"

His mischievous expression made her roll off the padded

table like a deflated balloon. Her face had turned a bright shade of red, and the unusual lack of clothing around her body created a surge of self-consciousness that had not been present since her last doctor's appointment.

The man laughed, his tattoos gleaming from too much moisturiser. "Did you have something else in mind?"

Rhiannon was shocked by his seductive tone. She held on tight to her small towel and tried to imagine the satisfying sound that her open palm would make against his solid cheekbones.

"You seriously need to relax," said Billy. "Besides, you're not my type anyway."

"And what is your type, exactly?"

"Beards, mainly. Really big ones."

This overload of personal information had come with surprising relief. It seemed that Rhiannon had nothing to worry about, after all.

She had already been weary enough about letting someone manhandle her like a piece of dough, especially a person with biceps as big as Billy. She hated going to the hairdressers, and if it weren't for her sore neck, she would usually never have been caught dead inside a health spa.

Now that she knew there were no alternative motives behind this highly intimate procedure, she made her way back to the table and let her cruel masseuse continue his torture.

"You don't get massages very often, do you?" asked Billy, as he inflicted even more punishment with his strong grip.

"How do you know that?"

"Cause you're as stiff as a board, darling."

Rhiannon huffed. She couldn't argue with that observation. For someone who spent most of her time behind a desk, she had more injuries than a blind skier.

"And as for your posture," he continued, "it's the worst I've ever seen."

"Yes, alright," said Rhiannon after another crack. "I didn't come here for a medical examination." She was just about to point out the man's own list of personal inadequacies, when she became reminded of the position of his hands around her tender calves. It would have been very unwise to upset him. Instead, she decided to change the subject: "You must be quite bored working here."

Billy chuckled. "How do you mean?"

"Well, I've barely seen a soul in this spa since I got here. And most of the people lurking around this hotel seem to be over eighty."

"You're never too old for a bit of pampering. Good for the circulation."

Rhiannon groaned. Her hamstrings did not agree.

"But, yeah, I get your point. It's like a graveyard around here at the moment," Billy continued. "Suits me just fine though. Easiest job I've ever had, actually. And the pay's pretty decent. Can't see it lasting much longer, though."

"Why's that?"

"Like you said: the place is dead. I'm no business expert, but it doesn't take a genius to work out that this hotel's not making money. It's been like this since I got here. If a hotel isn't busy during the summer, then when is it?"

"Argh!"

Rhiannon's scream didn't seem to faze the trainer in the slightest, and he continued to work his way further up her quad muscles.

"If it weren't for that American bloke living here, I'm sure we'd be in real trouble."

"I assume you're referring to Mr Fletcher," said Rhiannon, trying her best to breathe through the pain.

"Good old Fletch," said Billy. "I quite liked the bloke to be fair. Barmy as anything, though." He lifted up his victim's leg as though he were reaching the end of a wrestling match. "I guess money drives you crazy in the end. You know he used to go on about buying this hotel? Can you believe that?"

The pain now circulating around the journalist's body was momentarily numbed. This unexpected piece of hearsay was a welcome distraction.

"That's the first I've heard about that," she replied. "I thought he was just staying here until he found somewhere else."

Billy shook his head. "He told me himself. The guy wasn't modest, and it's amazing what people tell you when they're at their most vulnerable. Said he wanted to rescue the place before it's too late."

"How much money did he think he had? People don't just go around buying old castles."

"Don Fletcher wasn't your usual kind of guy."

Rhiannon thought about what the concierge had said about the will. Gethin seemed quite adamant that Don had intended to make a donation with his fortune, and from what she was hearing now, there was a lot more to that fortune than she had realised.

"Do you really think he had enough money to buy this place?" she asked.

The trainer shrugged. "I was his masseuse, not his accountant. But the bloke was definitely worth a few bucks."

"I can't imagine a psychic medium makes *that* much money."

"Are you kidding? They're just glamorised fortune tellers." Billy lifted up a towel and hovered it across the bottom half of his face. "Those guys have been swindling people since the dawn of time. The big-timers like Don just took it to a whole other level. Nah, he was filthy rich that one, and everyone around here knew it."

Once again, the thought of Don Fletcher's last will and testament dangled away in the forefront of Rhiannon's mind. "*Everyone?*"

Billy lowered his face towards her and exposed a mouth full of unnaturally white teeth. "*Everyone.* And anyone who denies it are lying through their backsides. I saw the way people in this hotel tried to befriend him. Lonely old man with nobody to leave his money to — can't blame them for trying, right? Plus those yanks are great tippers."

Rhiannon was about to shrug, when a forceful pressure caused her to yelp out in pain. The crack that followed was the loudest so far and even the trainer couldn't help but wince.

Billy removed his hand from the inside of her shoulder blade and stretched out his wrists. "That was a good one!"

∽

THE LOBBY of the Balamon Hotel was its usual deserted-self when Rhiannon came wandering in. She limped her way across the chequered tiles, like a wounded knight who had lived to fight another day. Her entire body had been pulled and yanked, contorted into knots, until it no longer obeyed itself. Billy's dungeon of pain and suffering had been her first proper sports massage, and she knew with great certainty that it would likely be her last.

The only thing keeping her going now was the prospect of dinner and a strong glass of gin, followed swiftly by an early night with her glorious feather pillows.

Standing behind the reception desk was a flustered looking Liz Pugh, the hotel manager and heir to the Balamon throne. The woman with her flowery dress and enormous earrings waved her down as if she knew that her guest had no intention of stopping.

"Ah, Ms Williams!" she called out in her high-pitched voice.

Rhiannon grunted underneath her breath, as the manager scooted over to her. The sound of her giant heels reminded the reporter of a trotting horse with no sense of balance.

"What a pleasure to see you," said Liz. "I trust you're enjoying your stay with us?"

Her guest did everything she could to stand up straight, whilst rubbing at the sore shoulder that might never be the same again. "Oh, I'm having a wonderful time."

"Splendid! That really is just splendid." The flustered manager straightened out her dress and neatened up her hair. "I'm sorry if I seem a little rushed. We're a receptionist down today and it's absolute chaos."

Rhiannon looked around at the lack of activity in what would normally be the busiest spot in the hotel. "I'm sure you're rushed off your feet. Don't let me keep you."

She was just about to walk away, when the woman scooted round to block her path.

"Oh, don't even get me started! The wicked girl has really left us in the lurch today. She never showed up for her shift and won't even return my calls. If there's one piece of advice I can offer about running a business, it's never work with family. They'll only let you down in the end."

"Gwen never turned up?" Rhiannon could visualise the young woman's terrified face again as it had burst out of the sauna.

"Isn't it just disgraceful? I trusted that girl and she betrayed me in a heartbeat. She's just like her mother. Well, never again!" The manager lifted up a small card and handed it to her. "Now, enough of her. I wanted to give you this."

Her guest inspected what appeared to be an invitation.

"I'm having a little birthday celebration tomorrow night. I'd just love for you to attend. I've been planning it for weeks."

"Oh, well, I don't really —"

"It will be taking place, here, in the main dining hall. So there are no excuses not to attend!" Her sudden laugh sent a surge of pain through Rhiannon's already suffering body. "Everyone will be there. My staff are all very excited as you can imagine. I've made it absolutely mandatory that they all enjoy themselves — or they can find somewhere else to work!"

The second laugh was even louder than the first.

"Please do feel free to bring along that little friend of yours," Liz added.

Rhiannon smiled. The thought of Alun's horrified face when being told that he'd be attending a large social gathering was enough to make the whole endeavour worthwhile. "How do you know about my friend?"

As far as Rhiannon could recall, the manager had not been around during Alun's short visit, and she had certainly not introduced him.

Liz grinned, like a giddy child with a naughty secret. "I've got eyes and ears everywhere in this place, Ms Williams. There's not much that gets past me."

Rhiannon could do nothing but force out a smile in return. "Oh, I'm sure there's not."

Just as the two were about to part ways, the journalist felt one of her many burning questions rising up into her impatient mouth.

"Oh, Miss Pugh!" she called.

The manager turned around, delighted that someone had wanted to speak with her of their own accord. "Please, call me Liz."

"Okay, Liz," said Rhiannon, who couldn't wait to wipe away that nauseating smile. "I heard you had a robbery in this hotel recently?"

The last-minute question had achieved its desired outcome.

Liz Pugh's face darkened with immediate effect. "A robbery? What ever gave you that idea?"

The twinkle in the reporter's eye only seemed to upset her further. "What can I say — those eyes and ears you mentioned are very handy."

There was a short silence, before the manager realised that she had forgotten to maintain her usual tone of exuberating hospitality.

"I can assure you, Ms Williams, you will find no crimes of any sort in this hotel. All your belongings are as safe as can be."

The Mexican stand-off of fake smiles and cheery voices was broken with the reporter's surrendering nod. "Please — call me Rhiannon," she said and made the weary journey back to her room.

CHAPTER 12

When Rhiannon opened up her room door (after what was now her second night in the strangest hotel she had ever stayed in), she had expected to find only one person standing there to greet her.

Although Alun had provided his usual courtesy of messaging ahead before his early morning visit, he had not, however, been nice enough to disclose the fact that he was also going to be accompanied by an officer of the law.

"Good morning," said the police officer, his expression as lifeless as his haircut. "Are you Rhiannon Williams?"

The woman before him pulled her dressing gown tight and checked the hallway for any more unexpected visitors.

"Is this some sort of practical joke?" she asked, directing her question towards Alun. "It's a bit early for a stripper, isn't it?"

The policeman coughed into his hand. "I can assure you there will be no *stripping* of any kind, Ms Williams."

"Thank goodness for that."

"This is not a laughing matter in the slightest. In fact, I've come here about a very serious matter indeed."

"Oh," said Rhiannon. She could tell this man was going to be a barrel of laughs. "Well I suppose you better come in then."

She led them both inside the room. Her entire suitcase had been emptied across the floor, and it resembled the aftermath of an unfortunate laundromat explosion. Alun wasn't too surprised at the mess, although it still hurt him deep inside.

"I hope you're enjoying your stay," said Officer Gwent, having almost stepped in a plate of leftovers.

Rhiannon made herself comfy on the bed and decided not to offer the constable a seat. She disliked patronising police officers at the best of times and could sense this boring jobsworth with a lack of personality was not going to win her over.

"Unless you're here on behalf of the tourism board, Officer," she said, "I suggest you cut to the chase."

Officer Gwent cleared his throat again. He was used to commanding the utmost degree of fear and cooperation in the village of Tremor, and it seemed this woman with the bad attitude would not be intimidated.

"Very well," he muttered and took his position at the window. The flowery curtains on either side of him did nothing to help his serious image, and the emergence of his notebook didn't even bat an eyelid. "I'm told you've been acquainted with a Gwen Tudor?"

"Who?"

"You might know her better as a staff member at this hotel."

"Keep going."

It was now Alun's turn to cough. "The sauna..."

"Oh," said Rhiannon. "I see."

"Yes," agreed Officer Gwent. "Mr Hughes here tells me she gave the impression that someone was trying to harm her."

"*Did* he now?"

The furious stare that came in Alun's direction was the exact reaction he had expected. But it still tore through him like a ray gun.

Even the police officer could sense the tension, and he decided it was best to continue: "He tells me that you both intended to report it to the authorities immediately, but that Miss Tudor had insisted otherwise."

"Oh, I bet he did," Rhiannon muttered, her deathly stare as potent as ever.

"It was actually Rhiannon's idea for me to report this on our behalf," Alun chimed in. He was doing his best to repair the damaged trust, but it was not doing him any good. "It's my fault we didn't come to you sooner. We were put in a very difficult situation."

"Would Mr Hughes mind if I answer my own questions?" Rhiannon asked.

Officer Gwent was struggling to decide which direction to look, and he made an awkward pause before continuing.

"We take death threats very seriously, as you can imagine. Can you confirm, Ms Williams, that she told you that there had been letters sent to her? That she knew who was trying to threaten her?"

Rhiannon shrivelled into her duvet. The words that followed came struggling out of her mouth. "Yes. She did."

"And did you get a name?"

"She said she couldn't say. All she told us was that they work at this hotel."

"There's something else she mentioned," Alun added, trying not to look in Rhiannon's direction. He could feel the daggers grazing against the corner of his eye. "Gwen seemed to think it was the person she saw leaving Don Fletcher's room, moments before he was found dead. They were dripping in foamy water and had a pile of papers under their arm."

The police officer's pen was moving at a pace it had never moved before. His hand was almost trembling.

"This is quite serious," he said. "Quite serious, indeed."

Rhiannon bit down against her lip to stop the tongue inside her mouth from unleashing a remark she would later regret.

Officer Gwent was buzzing with excitement. Normally, he had very little to report when it came to new crimes, and he couldn't wait to see the look on his sergeant's face during their next meeting. But his moment of glory would have to wait just a little while longer. He might only have just begun to scratch the surface of this new mystery, and he wanted to make sure he had all his facts straight before taking the credit.

He turned to his two onlookers and tried to remain composed. "You've both made the right decision coming to me today."

"Glad we could both help," said Rhiannon, her words targeted in the direction of a sheepish looking accountant.

"I will have to continue this conversation with Gwen, herself," the officer continued. "It sounds like there's a lot more she needs to disclose before I can get to the bottom of all this. But I will get to it — mark my words!"

"Oh, I'm sure you're always getting to the *bottom* of things, Officer."

The man gave Rhiannon's comment a raised eyebrow. "Yes, well. I think that's all for now. But I'm sure we'll be speaking again, I have no doubt."

"Looking forward to it."

The moment that Officer Gwent left the room was the moment Alun had dreaded all morning. When the police officer finally closed the door, he was soon pounced on like a helpless antelope.

"What do you think you're playing at?" Rhiannon growled,

her hands shaking him by his perfectly ironed shirt. "I gave that girl my word!"

Alun tripped back against the wall and felt her weight pinning him to the old fashioned wallpaper. "We had to report it!"

"You mean *you* had to report it! Couldn't turn a blind eye for just once in your life, could you? Everything has to be accounted for!"

She watched him cower at the sight of her long fingernails and longed for him to fight back. Anything for the excuse to slap him. Ultimately, she knew he was right and, at that very moment, she hated him for it.

Alun was soon released, and it took him a while before he felt safe enough to speak again.

"You'll thank me if anything actually *does* happen to her."

He winced, as a furious Rhiannon turned back around in disbelief. "Are you serious?"

The conviction in her friend's voice disintegrated. "The last thing we need is to be withholding information in a murder case."

"There'll be another murder case soon if you don't stop talking about it," Rhiannon assured him. She went to pick up some clothes and headed to the bathroom.

Alun could hear the shower exploding to life and wondered whether that was his cue to leave.

Just as he reached for the door handle, he heard a voice calling him back: "I think we should start looking into that robbery the concierge was talking about."

The accountant paused and began making his way back towards the sound of running water.

"You think it's related to Don Fletcher's death?" he called out, feeling awkward about talking to a wall.

"I think there's a lot more going on in this hotel than people are letting on," she called back. "And I'm not talking about the resident ghosts."

Alun thought about Gwen's description of the supposed killer leaving the scene of the crime. There had been few clues on the person's appearance, but there *had* been a description on what they were carrying.

"There was something else stolen that night," he called. "The papers under the killer's arm: I've been trying to think what they could be. You definitely didn't find a manuscript in that room?"

The accountant jumped back in fright, as Rhiannon appeared in the bathroom door in nothing but a towel. It was the quickest shower he had ever seen.

"I searched every inch of that room," she said. "Pretty hard to miss a manuscript."

Alun began following her into the bathroom to continue their conversation, only for her to turn around and frown.

"Do you mind?" she asked.

"Oh! Yes, sorry — I didn't realise you were..."

He took the hint and dashed back into the other room.

"Why would someone drown an old, washed-up psychic and then steal his unfinished autobiography?" she continued, much to her listener's relief.

"Maybe there are details about the man's life that they don't want the world to know?" Alun asked.

"Or maybe it wasn't a manuscript at all. Gwen said *papers*. What other documents do people care about when a person dies?"

"You think it was a *will*?"

A fully clothed Rhiannon eventually marched back into the room. "Whatever it was, someone was willing to get their hands very wet that morning."

Her wet hair reminded Alun of his ex-girlfriend, and the

sound of the roaring hairdryer gave him a strange, nostalgic feeling inside.

∼

"Oh, it was just awful," said the woman whose face reminded Rhiannon of a nervous chicken.

Carys Roden continued to pace around the dining hall with her clipboard. The assistant manager had an incredible nack for exceeding a great deal of energy whilst, at the same time, achieving very little.

Preparations for Liz Pugh's birthday party seemed to be well underway, and the enormous room was now covered in an abundance of fairy lights and paper trimmings. The majority of the dining tables had been rearranged to create a large space, an area that Carys had referred to as the "boogie floor".

In the corner was a scruffy man with an extra-large t-shirt setting up the speakers. He grunted and grumbled whilst trying to unravel a web of knotted cables.

"I'll never forget the way his face just floated in the water like that," Carys continued. "My baths have never been the same since."

Alun and Rhiannon gave her a sympathetic nod. They watched as she checked the table layouts for a third time.

"If it's a bad time," said Rhiannon, "We can always come back."

"Oh, there's never a good time! It's a madhouse here today with this party. Liz is very particular with how she likes everything, and I'm determined not to let her down."

"Heaven forbid."

Rhiannon felt a nudge after her accidental remark.

"Did you manage to get a good look at the suicide letter?" Alun asked.

"Oh, don't even get me started," said Carys. "That's something else I'd rather forget. Suicide is always so tragic. Mr Fletcher was never the happiest of guests, but I never would have expected him to take his own life. God rest his soul."

"Did you have a chance to read it?" asked Rhiannon.

"Read? Oh, the letter! Yes, well — I skimmed it briefly. It was the first thing I saw, actually. Right before I checked that bathroom."

The mere mention of her last word caused her to snivel again.

"Was there anything in the letter that stood out?" asked Alun.

"Stood out?"

"You know, any details — any names, perhaps?"

"Well, it was a struggle to read, if I'm honest. The spelling was a bit atrocious, especially considering he was a writer. But he was obviously not in his right mind. And it looked to have been typed out using that old typewriter he used."

"Any misspellings in particular?"

"I beg your pardon?"

Even Rhiannon turned to him in surprise.

"Any common words that were *misspelt*?" Alun asked again.

The woman was not any more the wiser, but she did her best to answer: "Gosh, I couldn't say. I'm afraid my memory is absolutely terrible!" On that note, she turned her attention to a crate of wine bottles being carried in. "Oh! I've forgotten to order in the ice! I knew there was something... She'll kill me if the champagne isn't cold enough!"

The other two looked at each other, as she tried to remember her breathing.

"Uh, well we should probably not keep you too much longer, Mrs Roden," said Alun, noticing the arrival of a disco ball. "It looks like you've got quite a lot on your plate."

"But there is just one other thing," Rhiannon chimed in, as her associate had already started walking away. "Any ideas on what was stolen that night?"

Carys' mouth began twitching even more nervously than usual. "Oh, that's really not my place to say, I'm afraid."

"No? Then whose place exactly is it?"

The lip quivered again. Carys Roden had always been a bad liar. She could never work out whether it was her nerves or the fact that her mouth had a very bad habit of spouting things out beyond her control. That day, it might well have been both, as a person's name came gurgling out from the back of her throat.

CHAPTER 13

The excursion to the third floor had been a short one. It was a section of the hotel that few members of staff were permitted to visit, and a place where members of the public were forbidden altogether. This strict boundary had only made it all the more alluring to one guest in particular — a certain journalist with a personal disdain for rules and restrictions.

"Are you sure this is a good idea?" Alun asked, as they scaled the last step into the darkened hallway. It was a question he had become used to asking, and one that he always knew the answer to.

Rhiannon shrugged. "She said Angela would know more, didn't she?"

Alun sighed. Carys had indeed confirmed that her manager's elderly mother was the victim in this recent theft, but she had in no way given them permission to visit her living quarters. The topic of the robbery had seemed to make the assistant manager quite uncomfortable, and her attempt to deny all knowledge had resulted in an accidental name drop that Rhiannon had snapped up like a dog to a free biscuit.

"The birthday girl has gone out for the day," she added, "which I think is the perfect time to pay mummy a little visit."

The hallway was not that dissimilar to the ones below, only with less daylight and fewer doors (some of them with the appearance of having been closed for centuries). They followed a single oriental runner that seemed to go on forever, off into a distant darkness that made Alun want to reconsider their decision and turn back. The prospect of bumping into the hotel's supposed ghostly inhabitants had also entered his mind, although Rhod had assured him that they were a lot harder to come by during the daytime (and if you couldn't trust the word of a junior medium, then who could you?).

Paintings and ornaments were far more prevalent on this floor, and the faces of various generations of previous owners were all framed for the occasional passerby. Alun could feel the eyes of these acrylic men and women, none of which had chosen to smile. It wasn't often that these portraits got to witness newcomers to their floor. When it came to their personal lives, Liz Pugh and her mother had managed to create a cocoon of privacy within this secluded area of the hotel.

As the accountant and the journalist continued their walk among the shadows, they turned the next corner and were met with an abrupt dead-end.

"Is that it?" Rhiannon asked.

"Must be," said Alun, slightly relieved at the shortened journey.

They had been informed that Angela Pugh's quarters were located through the final door, a piece of information that the assistant manager had regretted letting slip from the moment it had escaped her loose lips. After years of interviewing the most introverted of individuals, Rhiannon had become an expert in prying out the tiniest details with even the most innocent sounding questions. Carys Roden's overactive tongue had been like an open buffet of knowledge (or at least a very specific type of knowledge). She wasn't the brightest bulb in the chandelier, but her years of service at the *Balamon Hotel* meant that she knew more about the building than the journalist did.

"I suppose we should knock," Alun said, only to receive the usual type of glance that Rhiannon gave him in such a situation.

After lowering her raised eyebrow, she turned the handle and listened to the sweet sound of an unlocked door. On the other side was a room that dwarfed any of the ones on the floor below. Its ceiling was twice the size of Rhiannon's en suite, and the amount of floor space made all of her former London apartments look like a shoebox.

Despite an enormous window, the closed curtains had shut out any traces of natural light, and the only signs of life came from a flickering lantern in the middle of a cluttered dressing table. A vast collection of books seemed to have spilled out from a row of shelves and, along with the piles of clothes and jewellery, were starting to take over the entire room.

Alun gazed over at the unmade four poster bed and started to believe that perhaps Rhiannon was not the messiest person in the world, after all. The smell of dust in the air was enough to induce a panic attack, and just when his adrenaline levels had reached a record high, the sight of a long tail, curling around his leg, sent him leaping into the air with a cry.

The sight of the furry culprit — a black and white cat called Seimon — did nothing to calm his nerves, and the hope of any sympathy had been dashed by Rhiannon's amused laugh.

"You're scaring him," she said, a comment that Alun had hoped was directed towards the cat.

In all the commotion, the two trespassers had failed to notice the silent figure sitting in an old armchair. Beside it was a fireplace that had been dead since the winter months, although, judging by the person's pale complexion, it looked as if some warmth was severely needed.

"You're too late for breakfast and too early for lunch," said the woman. "Don't they teach people how to read a clock anymore?"

She reached out her skeletal hands, as Seimon the cat went leaping onto her lap.

"Angela Pugh, I take it?" Rhiannon asked, the playfulness in her face quickly dissipating.

"Mrs Pugh, to you, young lady."

The journalist was mildly flattered. Despite the authoritative tone and belittling intent, any description involving the word *young* was perfectly fine with her. It was not an adjective she heard very often.

"Forgive us, Mrs Pugh," said Alun. "But we're not members of the hotel staff."

The frail woman squinted at him with her lifeless eyes. She wasn't so sure about the woman with the attitude, but the well-groomed man in smart clothes seemed alright.

"You'll have to come closer if you want me to hear you, lad," she said. "If you're not here to work, young man, then why are you here?"

Alun blushed. It was that word again: *young*. Flattery would get her everywhere, the accountant thought.

"We heard you had a robbery here recently," Rhiannon answered.

The older woman was struck by a glimmer of disappointment. If that obnoxious girl with the terrible dress sense didn't wind her neck in soon, she thought, there was a good cane in the nearby wardrobe with her name on it.

"Ah, I see. So they've sent more of you, have they? Fat lot of use that will do. If your police work so far is anything to go by, then that thief will never get caught. It's been almost a week, and I'm yet to have my husband's medals returned."

And just like that, a streak of light had been shed. Rhiannon could never predict how a line of questioning would go, but she sensed this one was going to be quite productive.

"The medals?" she asked.

"Don't play the fool with me," Angela snapped. "What else would I be talking about?"

Alun could feel the anger building up into the base of his friend's forehead. It was the appearance of a certain vein along the side of her neck that had always been the giveaway. It had served as a useful warning signal on many occasions.

"I think my associate is just trying to clarify a few facts, Mrs Pugh," he said. "We would appreciate hearing your own account of the incident." The vein slowly began to subside but was subject to return at any moment.

The woman stroked her cat and took another glance at the nice man's shoes, as they took a step towards her. "Please, call me Angela."

Rhiannon let out a scoff which she had made no attempt to restrain.

"Thank you, Angela," said Alun with another step. "If you could please just refresh us on a few things. At what point did you notice that someone had stolen from you?"

"When I woke up to feed Seimon," said Angela. "Whoever it was who had snuck in during the middle of the night and had taken the entire safe." She shuddered. "It makes me sick to think that this criminal was creeping around in this very same room."

"Was the door locked?" Rhiannon asked.

"Of course it wasn't. A person doesn't expect to be robbed by her own hotel staff."

"What makes you think it was one of the staff?"

"How else would they know I had anything worth stealing? And why would someone purposely make their way to this very room — of all the rooms? I thought you were supposed to be a police officer?"

"Let's get back to the safe," said Alun, deciding it was a very good moment to interject. "Was it a decent size?"

"It was small enough to fit under there," replied Angela, pointing towards the small dressing table.

The accountant looked over towards the gap underneath. With a pair of drawers on either side, it was barely two feet in width.

"So small enough for an able-bodied person to carry."

"Unless you're a weakling like me, then, yes. It wasn't heavy and probably the size of a typewriter."

"A typewriter?" Rhiannon asked, surprised at the choice of comparison.

The woman glared at her with those stern eyes. "Yes. A *typewriter.*"

Alun chimed in again to break the awkward silence: "Was there anything in there other than the medals?"

"A few pieces of jewellery. But I don't care about them. It's the medals that are really valuable. They belonged to my late husband."

Alun nodded. "Sir Dylan Pugh. I'm sure they hold a lot of memories."

"They're worth a lot of money too. One of those medals is a Victoria Cross. They're worth an absolute fortune."

"Sounds like anything comes with a price these days," Rhiannon muttered. "Even heroic acts."

"I beg your pardon?" Angela snapped.

"It must have been very hard losing your husband," Alun said in a rush of panic. "I can only imagine the grief of losing a loved one."

"Yes," Angela agreed. She kept her threatening stare fixed on the journalist. "It was very hard."

"It can't have been easy being a stepmother, either," said Rhiannon. The accountant braced himself for the worst. "Am I right in thinking Dylan's eldest daughter, Rowena, was an only a child when you married her father?"

"That is none of your business."

"I only see one daughter around now. Liz is Dylan's second child but your first, am I right?"

Alun clutched his own face and waited for the inevitable.

"What on earth does this have to do with my stolen valuables? How dare you come in here and bring up my personal life! You are the worst police officer I have ever met in my life."

"Police officer?" Rhiannon asked. She moved closer to the furious old woman and unleashed a smug grin. "We never said we were *police officers*..."

Angela's eyes widened to expose some red veins on the outer edges. "Help!" she cried, banging her hands against the chair. "Help! I'm being abducted by a pair of criminals!"

Her loud screeching sent a rattled Alun stumbling towards her, his arms flailing in the air, desperate for her to stop.

"No, no! We're not here to hurt you! We just came to talk!"

His pleading only made the elderly woman worse, and just as he approached her chair, she lifted up a spare cane and began swiping at him as if he were a pesky wasp.

"Get away! You evil, little man!"

After feeling the wrath of her cane, the beaten accountant turned around to his friend for help. Rhiannon stood there watching, almost enjoying this performance of *Punch and Judy*.

"I think it's time we made a move, don't you?" she said with a smile.

Alun couldn't agree more, and soon the two trespassers were scurrying off back down the hallway at twice the speed they had moved on the way up. As they made their way back down the creaking staircase, back to the safety of the second floor, Rhiannon paused at the sight of something very intriguing.

"What are you stopping for?" Alun cried. "We need to keep moving!"

"Look," she replied, her attention focused on a single door at the bottom of the stairs. "You know whose room that is?"

Her friend reluctantly backed himself up, until he was on the exact same step. Despite his desperate rush to get as far away as he could from the woman on the third floor, the view from the staircase was as intriguing as she had promised.

"That's Don Fletcher's room," he said.

The journalist nodded. "Now if Gwen was not supposed to be in the hotel that morning, why was she in this corner of the building?" The pause from Alun was enough to signal she had made her point. "There are only two positions you could have seen someone coming out of Don's room: either you had to be heading towards the third floor, along the second floor hallway, or…"

"She was coming down from the third floor…"

They both looked at each other with a knowing stare.

"Why would Gwen be interested in the third floor?" Alun asked.

Rhiannon smiled. "I think that's exactly what Don's killer was wondering."

CHAPTER 14

Johnny Roberts recognised his father's silhouette from the moment he peered through the glass. He would recognise it anywhere: the pointed nose, the large chin and even larger body. It reminded him of an Alfred Hitchcock profile, only a more crooked and hunched over version.

Gwyn Roberts had never forgiven his sons for bringing him to the cruel prison that he called *Plas Madog*. The nursing home had a thriving community of local residents, which only disturbed the elderly man even further. Every face in that building was nothing more than a blast from the past, as he had lived in the town of Tremor for the entire duration of his life. He had buried every grandmother, every parent, every uncle. He had seen them all weep and cry until their loved one was finally put to rest by his own capable hands.

But those days were long gone, and the retired undertaker had faced the inevitable reality that the next funeral would likely be his own. Despite being bound to a wheelchair that many others had sat in before him, he still held out hope that he would someday escape the confines of *Plas Madog*'s walls by his own accord. All he needed was a small window of time, a brief lapse in concentration from one of the patronising care workers. That day would come, and when it did, Gwyn Roberts would be ready.

His son Johnny continued to watch him through the glass, his angry lawn mower growling beneath his feet. The old man appeared to be more vacant than usual that afternoon. He wondered what poisonous thoughts were lurking in that bald head of his and suspected that there might not have been any thinking going on whatsoever. His father had not uttered a single word to him during the last visit and felt that the harsh silent treatment was probably for the best.

Once his last job for the afternoon had been completed, Johnny silenced the mower and headed inside. Passing through the small staff room, he was surprised to see some new faces. The turnover of employees was notoriously high at *Plas Madog* with many having grossly underestimated the exhausting life of working in a nursing home.

"Afternoon, Johnny!" Louisa called. "There's still an open spot if you want to join us."

Johnny washed his hands and gave the manager a playful wink.

"Nah, you're alright, Louisa. I don't think the old man could stomach me everyday. Plus I don't have the patience you lot have."

"Suit yourself," said Louisa. "Your dad seems in good spirits today. He's been wanting to speak to you all morning. I think he's really settling in with us."

"Is that right? I always knew he'd come round in the end."

Moments later, and the young man was already regretting the visit.

"There's something very sinister going on around here," said Gwyn, his beady eyes scanning the entire room.

"You can say that again," his son agreed, whilst munching on the older man's uneaten roast dinner. "This gravy's very suspicious." He took another whiff of the brown liquid dripping from his fork and tried not to gag.

"I'm not talking about the food," his father hissed. He peered again at all his fellow residents and their unassuming carers. "Something's not right. I think we're being drugged."

Johnny sat back in his chair and yawned. "I'm sure over half the people in here are on drugs."

"Not those kind of drugs, you fool. I'm talking about ones that affect the mind." He placed a firm finger against his temple. "Our biggest asset. They're trying to steal it from us and turn us into mindless zombies."

"I don't think you need drugs for that."

His father grabbed his plate and threw the contents at him.

"I knew you'd be too stupid to understand!" he barked. "If you had any wits about you, my business wouldn't be in so much trouble. You wouldn't be cutting grass like some jobless gardener!"

The topic of work had touched a nerve. It wasn't the gravy all over his shirt or the peas across his lap that bothered Johnny, but the criticism of his ability to run a family company. Little did his father know, but he was doing everything in his power to help their legacy continue, something the previous generation would never have had the nerve to do.

"Who said the business was in trouble?" Johnny asked, scooping up a handful of peas and stuffing them in his mouth.

"I hear things."

"Heard things from who?" The pause said it all. "My brother's been round here running his mouth off again, has he? Shame he doesn't have the gall to say it to my face."

Gwyn had always been protective over his youngest son. Unlike Johnny, he had been a far more sensitive child, and the world was a harsh place for sensitive people. There had been times he had wished Rhod had been the eldest. A business needed a cautious mind and a trustworthy soul — not a reckless owner who trampled over everything in his path. Deep down, he loved them both. But it had been death, not love, that had always paid the bills.

The old man grumbled his way to a response. "He tells me you're putting in shifts over at the Balamon now."

"So what?"

"You're telling me business is booming when you're working extra jobs?"

Johnny grinded his teeth and thought about all the ways he could punish his younger brother for opening his big mouth.

"No harm in making a few extra bob on the weekend."

"Back when I was running that place, there was no time for weekends. What's changed?"

The younger man shrugged. "People are living longer."

"Nonsense!" Gwyn leaned forward and almost toppled himself over in the process. His son observed that crooked finger, pointing at him, as it had done countless times before. He felt a lecture coming on. "You've not maintained that personal touch — those close relationships with the people of this town. That's how you get their business. They need to trust you. They need to choose you over any other competition."

Johnny was prodding away at a piece of meat with his toothpick. It had been bothering him for the whole conversation.

"It's a little pointless if they're dead," he muttered.

"That's *exactly* why you've been failing!" Gwyn cried. "It's not the deceased you should be interested in — it's the people still alive — the friends and family! A local business is about building relationships." He pointed around the room. "Take this place for example: I know everything about every person in this room. I know Tony has a daughter with a heart problem. I know

Nerys Wilkinson has just been diagnosed as a type one diabetic. I know Lesley Price had a dog called Lemon. Why do I know all this? Because you never quite know when you need a person's help."

Both of their faces were now almost touching.

"I'm perfectly capable of helping myself. Unlike some people..."

He turned their attention to the wheelchair, and his father could see that he might as well have been talking to a brick wall. The stare had been long enough that even the staff had noticed.

Johnny was now ready to deliver a blow he knew would hurt the man: "Shame you never used this philosophy at home. Those were the only relationships that really mattered."

The mounting tension was smashed to pieces by the sound of a crashing mug. Johnny and his father unlocked their horns and took notice of the commotion happening to their left.

"You stupid girl!" screeched an elderly woman in a nightgown. "You know I'm lactose intolerant!"

Angharad, a carer in her early twenties began clearing up a shattered mug that had been full of tea.

"I'll get you another one," Angharad said, her tone resembling that of someone as broken inside as the hot drink.

Gwyn observed the scene with a grave shaking of his head. "That poor girl won't last the week at this rate. She's only been here three days and they're walking all over her."

Johnny stretched out his arms and climbed to his feet.

"I fancy a brew myself," he said. "You still on the sweeteners?"

His father gave a reluctant nod. "Only if I want to see my next birthday." He contemplated for a moment. "On second thoughts... make it two sugars."

Johnny was about to walk away, when something made him pause and turn around.

"Who did you say was diabetic again?" he asked.

"What's it to you?" the older man grumbled.

His son let out a giant grin. "Just trying to take an interest in my community."

Over in the kitchen, Angharad was frantically tossing tea bags into a tray of mugs. Johnny entered with a chirpy swagger, embracing the chaos going on around him, as other care workers passed in and out.

"Need a hand?" he asked her.

The young woman barely looked up but seemed to appreciate the offer. She began pointing at the various mugs, her mind desperately trying to remember the order.

"That's for Mr Humphreys — black, one sugar — this one's for Mrs Neale, coffee, extra milk — oh, and that one there is Nerys Wilkinson — milk, two sweeteners — no sugar! She's diabetic."

The undertaker smiled and placed a reassuring hand on her shoulder. "Don't you worry. I'll take care of these for you."

Angharad wiped the sweat from her brow and gave him an appreciative nod. She took a deep breath, grabbed the first tray and set off with the first load.

Having been left alone with the second tray, Johnny hopped and skipped around the kitchen before grabbing a freshly boiled kettle. Next, he went straight for the bag of sugar on the table and began shovelling over half a dozen spoonfuls of sweet, white grains into a single mug. The mischievous tea maker whistled away, as he made the most sugary cup of tea known to man.

He stirred his teaspoon and muttered under his breath: "I hope you like it sweet, Mrs Wilkinson."

CHAPTER 15

Alun passed through the gates of the *Balamon Hotel* and checked his watch. He had allowed plenty of time for his walk from Tremor, and it seemed that he had completed the journey in record time. Covered in a layer of sand and dirt, his favourite dress shoes had paid a hefty price for an evening hike, and the patches of dust along the bottom of his trousers would be bothering him for the rest of the night.

Nevertheless, it had almost been worth it for the spectacular sunset, and with a good half hour up his sleeve before the party (he had no intention of being early, especially for a large social gathering), he decided that a nice wander around the gardens would be in order.

His knowledge of plants was extremely limited, but even Alun could appreciate the Japanese garden he had discovered nestled in the far corner of the grounds. The exotic looking flowers and carefully arranged stones created a moment of calm and tranquillity. He had never quite understood the concept of "zen" and "mindfulness" (a darn good session of bank reconciliations was normally more than enough to calm his spirit), but, standing amongst this small haven of peace and quiet, the accountant might almost have gone as far to say that he felt "at one" with the place.

Despite the questionable condition of the hotel's interiors, Alun was surprised to find that its gardens were very much in pristine order. The lawns were freshly mowed, its hedges had been trimmed back and any weeds had been fully eradicated.

It wasn't until he entered the seclusion of the walled garden that he discovered who the culprit behind this incredibly high standard of groundwork actually was.

As he followed the sound of running water, through the rows of flourishing tomato plants, he stumbled upon a Victorian glasshouse. Through the steamed glass was a figure moving around inside, and when he reached the doorway, the mysterious gardener stepped into view with a suspicious frown.

"Can I help you?" he asked, the hosepipe in his hand still dripping.

"Oh, I didn't mean to disturb you," Alun said. "I was just having a look around."

The bearded man smiled and went to turn off the water. "Not at all! Anyone who appreciates the wonder of the great outdoors is always welcome here. A fellow gardener, are you?"

"Uh, well, I wouldn't say —"

"Yes, I thought as much. I know a fellow shrub enthusiast when I see one. Have you been down the Japanese garden yet?"

"Uh, yes. I have, actually."

The gardener beamed with pride. "That's my own personal favourite, that one. Took me years to put it together. I saw one on telley and became obsessed. I kept telling Mrs Pugh it was worth the trouble."

"That was Liz Pugh, I take it?"

"Lizzie? Good grief — no! She was knee-high back then. I'm talking about her mother, Angela. Showing my age now, aren't I?"

He placed a grubby hand on Alun's shoulder and walked him back outside. The accountant tried hard not to think about the dirt seeping into his dinner jacket.

"Come," said the old gardener, "I'll show you the orchard. I'm Robin, by the way."

The muddy hand was soon clasped around Alun's own hand. He grimaced and reluctantly shook it. "I'm Alun."

"You're looking very smart, if you don't mind me saying."

"I'm here for the party."

A sudden terror washed over Robin's face. "Oh, good Lord — the party! Is that tonight?"

Alun nodded.

"Oh, dear," Robin continued. "I'd completely forgotten. I'm so glad you came. I'll have to throw a shirt on. Lizzie would never talk to me again if I missed it."

The man began smelling his own armpits and seemed happy with the verdict.

"You've known her for a long time, then?" asked Alun, gazing at the passing flowers, most of which he could never have named but still admired their beauty.

"Her whole life!" The gardener laughed. "I've been around here a long, long time, as you can see. I might as well be part of the architecture. I'm one of the oldest fossils in this here garden!"

"What was Dylan Pugh like?"

"He was the finest boss you could ever work for! A proper gentleman. Just like his father before him. Working for him was a true honour."

"Did you get to meet his first wife?"

Robin lowered his head with a grave expression. "Ah, yes... dear, old Maggie. God bless her soul. Jumped from a top floor window, you know? Was a huge shock to everyone at the time. Suicide is a horrible thing."

"Yes," said Alun, his mind whirling. "People are very unpredictable."

"Then Angela came along, of course. Couldn't have been more different." He leant in and kept his voice down. "If I'm being really honest, she wasn't very well liked around here when she first arrived."

Alun thought about his encounter with the woman earlier that day. "I can't possibly imagine why."

"The staff were horrified when Sir Dylan announced their engagement. Then there was poor young Rowena..."

"Dylan's eldest daughter?"

Robin nodded. "She hated her stepmother with a passion. As soon as her father died, she wanted nothing more to do with this place. I still see her around the village from time to time, and it's always nice to catch up."

They approached a door at the edge of the walled garden, and when it opened, Alun was introduced to an enormous apple orchard.

"This is another one of my pride and joys," said the gardener. "It was in a right state when I arrived, but I'm given free reign to do what I want with the apples. I even make my own cider now."

He plucked one of the succulent looking apples and threw it towards his visitor.

"Go on! Give it a try!"

Alun caught it and gave the fruit a quick wipe against his shirt. Robin waited for the crunch and received a satisfied nod.

The two men shared a comfortable silence, as both of them munched on their freshly picked apples.

"What is Maggie short for?" Alun eventually asked, once his mouth was no longer filled with pulp.

"I beg your pardon?"

"Sir Dylan's first wife. I presume it's Margaret."

"Uh, yes. That's right. I've always known her as Maggie, I suppose. Why do you ask?"

The accountant brushed his hand through the tree leaves and felt a whole new appreciation for the miracle of horticulture. After the lingering air of death within the hotel walls, it was refreshing to find so much life on the outside.

"No reason. Just curious. This is the second suicide I've come across in this hotel. It must be more common than I thought."

Robin studied him whilst chewing on the final pieces of his apple. "Ah, yes," he said. "You're referring to our old friend, Mr Fletcher. That was another tragic event. I'd never linked the two, to be honest."

"There might be no link at all," said Alun. "My brain has a tendency to look for patterns. I think it's all those years of scanning through accounting ledgers."

"Accountant, are you? Well, I never. My uncle was an accountant." Robin smirked and tapped the back of his own head. "Never inherited any of *those* genes, mind. Numbers give me a bit of a migraine."

They left the enclosure of apple trees and returned to the walled garden. The sun had continued to fall, and in the time they had visited the orchard, the light had diminished into a garden of mysterious shadows.

"So how do you know about old Don Fletcher, then?" Robin asked.

"I never knew him personally," said Alun. "But he's sort of the reason I'm over here, I suppose. It sounds like he made quite the impression on people in this hotel."

Robin seemed almost amused. "Well, that's one way of putting it. He was a bit different, that's for sure. Wasn't like anyone else I ever knew, and I met the bloke on two separate visits."

The hotel loomed behind him, its windows now glowing

underneath the darkened sky. These lines of orange glows were like eyes, peering at them, watching their every move.

"*Two* visits?" Alun asked.

"Oh, yes," said the gardener. "This recent tenure of his was not the first time Mr Fletcher graced us with his presence. The first time was in the late seventies." He performed a deep stretch of his tired neck. "We were both a lot younger then."

Alun scratched his head and hoped he wasn't being bitten by something. "But what was he doing here then?"

Robin shrugged. "Same thing he was trying to do this time, probably: looking for things that go bump in the night." He took another look around to make sure that they were alone. "Although, his attention wasn't always on the ghosts. It was well known back then that he and her lady ship were... you know... *cross-pollinating*, as we like to call it."

His listener dropped his mouth in shock. "Are you really suggesting that Don Fletcher and Angela Pugh were... having an *affair*?"

"I'm not just suggesting. It was pure fact among the staff. They'd been caught a number of times, although they'd always deny it. But you can't keep secrets around here for very long."

The gardener checked his watch. "Oh, blimey," he said. "I'd better get my skates on. You know the way back to the house?"

Alun nodded, still bemused by the scandalous news (or old news, apparently).

"I'll see you over there, then!"

Robin scurried off with a skip in his step and a jolly whistle.

It was almost time to attend the party, and Alun would have much preferred an early night with a cup of camomile tea. He dusted off his trousers, used a leaf to wipe down his shoes and made the short journey back to the front entrance.

The hotel lights brightened as he approached the building, and it seemed like many of the guests had already arrived. What was normally a deserted car park was filled with all manner of different vehicles, and their owners were all flocking to the front door in bright and elegant evening wear.

One figure lurked in the background, watching and smoking, as they walked by. It was Gethin, the concierge, and his keen eye immediately spotted an approaching Alun.

"Didn't expect to see you here," he said, after finishing off his cigarette and joining him on a stroll through the foyer. "She managed to drag you to this thing as well, then?"

"Something like that," said Alun, having tried to avoid the extra company.

"It's the same every year," said Gethin. "Your lady ship makes it mandatory for all staff to attend, including the volunteers. I suppose that's what you do when you don't have any friends. I guess that's what you are now: her new friend."

"Oh, I'm sure she's just being polite. Rhiannon and I thought it would be good to show our faces."

The concierge chuckled to himself. "Nah, you're well in her pocket now. You'll be going on coffee dates and God knows what before you know it." He pulled out a silver flask from his inside pocket and took a swig. "Still, we might as well make the best of it, eh?"

He offered up a swig, but his new wingman firmly declined. Alun had never liked the man since the moment they had first met, and his opinion had yet to change.

"Suit yourself," said Gethin. "But it'll be a long night for you." The man let out a wicked grin. "Wouldn't it be great if something really fun happened? Like a big food fight or a drunken brawl — something to really ruin the birthday girl's night."

"Is there something you have planned?" asked Alun, trying his best to humour the man.

Personally, he was quite happy for it to be the most

uneventful evening possible. He was also looking forward to finding Rhiannon. If he was going to brave the horrors of a party, it was going to be a lot easier with her by his side.

The sound of laughter and music filled his ears, and a sudden jitter of nerves slipped into his empty stomach. It was time to enter the lion's den.

In an unusual display of thoughtfulness, Gethin opened up the final door to let him through, and they were met with a hall full of people.

Despite the forced circumstances of most of the partygoers there, everyone seemed to be having a good time. The atmosphere had been improved dramatically from the empty hollowness of the morning preparations, and the excessive decorations and lights were now complemented by the addition of life and soul.

Turning to his right, Alun saw that he had already been ditched by the chatty concierge, and he was now left to fend for himself among a sea of curious eyes. He roamed through the floor of beaming staff members, some of them he recognised from around the hotel. Such an environment had always made him feel strangely alone, as though he were an invisible ghost wandering among the living. He wished he could play along and pretend that he was having a good time, but his terrified face would never allow it.

When he reached the welcoming sanctuary of the large drinks table, he came across something that almost floored him quicker than an entire bottle of tequila. Standing over at the other end of the table were two people who appeared to be sharing a hysterical joke. The chemistry between them was undeniable, and they looked at each other in a way that filled the accountant with terror.

Desperate to crawl under the table to hide, he heard his name being shouted out by a familiar voice.

"Alun!"

Rhiannon waved at him, before continuing to chuckle and flirt with the handsome young man beside her. Alun waved back, as he briefly made eye contact with her new friend: a playful and intoxicated Johnny Roberts.

CHAPTER 16

Alun loitered by the drinks table, sipping on his gin and tonic. He was a lost puppy in a kennel of wild dogs, and he wished someone would come over there and rescue him.

Rhiannon, on the other hand, seemed to be having a wonderful time. She was also seizing the opportunity of getting to know a certain charismatic groundworker (one who Alun could have sworn he had also seen dressed as a funeral director).

Alun scanned the enormous room full of people and was surprised to find a person who looked almost as miserable as he did. Crouched like a lonely gargoyle in the far corner was Rhod. These two antisocial outcasts caught each other's stare and exchanged a polite nod.

Bored and out of place, the teen was pleased to see the awkward man in grubby shoes crossing the room to join him.

"Fancy seeing you here," said Rhod.

"Likewise," said Alun, having polished off the last of his drink. "How are you enjoying the party?"

"I've had more fun hanging out in graveyards."

"Well that doesn't surprise me."

They observed the merriment going on around them and shared the same disgust.

"I'd tell your girlfriend to be careful there," said Rhod, turning their attention to Rhiannon and Johnny, who continued their banter with remarkable ease.

"Oh, she's not my girlfriend," said Alun, his throat turning dry.

Rhod couldn't help but appear cynical. "Really? Then what are you then?"

"Uh, it's a good question, actuality. I often try to define the relationship myself. I suppose you could say we're like... colleagues, or — friends. That's right, we're friends."

"Well she seems to be getting along very well with my brother."

"Ah, your brother. That makes sense." Alun tried to hide his discomfort at the blossoming conversation going on before them. "I'm sure they just have a lot in common."

"It's doubtful," said Rhod. "My brother's a very unusual man."

Alun was about to point out that "unusual" seemed to be a Roberts family trait, but he didn't want to make the young man more downhearted than he already was.

He decided to turn his attention to other members of the crowd. Some of them he recognised: Gethin, the concierge; Carys, the assistant manager; Robin, the gardener. But there were many he had yet to meet.

"I assume you know most of the people in here," he said.

"I'm familiar with everyone," said Rhod. "I wouldn't say I really *know* anyone. If I did, I wouldn't be standing here on my own."

"That's a good enough start."

The curious teenager turned to look at him.

"Let us remove the idea of a deceased killer for now," Alun

continued. "And focus on the living. If you had to pick your number one suspect — the person most likely to have drowned a helpless Don Fletcher — who would it be?"

Rhod took a deep breath, and his eyes flashed with a rush of excitement. What a question, he thought, but it was one he relished in trying to answer. "Wow... where do I start? There's the people who openly hated him like Mark, the hotel chef; that concierge, who hates everybody..."

"What about the people he got along with?"

"Why would they matter?"

Alun watched as a young woman in the distance was showing off her bracelet. "You don't leave your inheritance to people you don't like."

The teenager nodded and accepted it was a fair point. "Well, he spent a lot of time with Billy from the spa. But that was only cause he had a bad back. Then there's that housekeeper who used to get him his morphine."

The man next to him listened to every word with great concentration. Just like Officer Gwent, he jotted down the facts — only not in a notebook — but in the secure cortex of his brain.

"The housekeeper's name is Mared, isn't it?" he asked.

"She's over there," said Rhod and pointed to the young woman with fiery, red hair. She swayed to the music in a moment of careless bliss.

The alcohol in the room was in full flow, and many of the partygoers seemed to be gradually losing their inhibitions. Any preconceived notions that they were merely attending a mandatory work function had started to fade, and the atmosphere had become quite lively.

Most people had even missed the arrival of a reluctant Angela Pugh, who slipped into the room in her rickety wheelchair. Her sour face revealed everything anyone would need to know about her stance on the event.

"I didn't expect to see *her*," Alun remarked, the memory of his visit to the third floor still raw in his mind.

"It's not often she shows her face," said Rhod.

"The old crow's down from her nest I see," added a slurring voice. Alun and Rhod both turned to see the concierge standing there beside them. "That must mean the birthday girl can't be too far behind. Lucky us!"

Gethin sipped away on his whiskey and continued to give the elderly woman a disgusted stare. The other two were surprised he had joined them. If he was willing to associate himself with a pair of social outcasts like them, then he must have been less popular than Alun had thought.

"Get a look at the state of her," continued Gethin. He was now observing Mared, who appeared to be laughing hysterically and twirling around in her bohemian dress. "I don't know what she's wearing, but I've seen more subtlety at a pantomime. Guess you can't expect any class from the likes of her."

Just as the oblivious housekeeper was about to laugh again, she caught the dirty look coming her way. It was all she needed.

"You got something to say?" she asked, having marched her way across the room. "Or did you just want a photograph?"

The concierge smiled and put an arm around a nervous Alun. "We were actually having a private conversation," he sneered. "But I'm not surprised you want to make it all about *you*."

Mared quivered with rage, causing the pint of murky liquid in her hand to jiggle. His smug grin had only made it worse.

"What is your problem?" she asked. "You've always had it in for me since I started!"

"Now mind your manners," said Gethin. "You're forgetting I outrank you in this hotel."

The young woman moved closer, her eyes as wide as a barn owl. "You think I'm scared? You might be able to bully everyone else around here, but I couldn't care less. I'll show you exactly where you can shove your precious rank!"

Alun was getting more and more worried by the second. His unintentional association with the poisonous concierge was making him want to push the man away. Rhod had already made himself scarce and was witnessing the argument from the safety of the buffet table.

"If you really want to know," Gethin continued, "we were discussing the lack of class around here. Some of us know how to look respectable." He gazed down at her unique dress and made his disapproval quite clear.

Mared took the hint, and she lunged forward in a fit of rage.

Unlike the nimble concierge, who leapt out of the way like a startled deer, Alun was left behind to receive an entire pint of rum and coke across his face. Wiping off a layer of sticky liquid from his eyes, he saw the crowd of gawking faces, including a shocked Rhiannon and her amused new friend.

"Oh! I'm so sorry!"

Mared's cries of regret did little to wash away the humiliation, as did the handful of napkins that she used to try and wipe him down.

Dry as a bone and revelling in his near escape, Gethin stood back to enjoy the housekeeper's moment of panic. "Like I said, you can't expect anything less from trash like that."

Just as Mared prepared for another attack, this time with an empty pint glass and a clenched fist, the whole room turned its attention to the grand entrance of Liz Pugh.

The hired disk jockey had switched from his usual selection of eighties pop music to an over-the-top fanfare of trumpets and drums. He then lifted up his microphone and prepared to do the honours: "Ladies and gentlemen, please give a warm welcome to our marvellous birthday girl!"

An ecstatic Liz Pugh leaped up and down, oblivious to the rather underwhelming round of applause. She twirled around in her enormous, colourful dress, which eminded Alun of a sixties lampshade that his mother once owned.

The birthday girl was soon approached by the hired photographer and any nearby bystanders were swiftly pulled in for a happy snap.

"Someone likes attention," Rhiannon muttered.

Johnny shrugged beside her and lifted up his beer. "As long as she's buying then I'd happily dance her round the room."

"Off you go then." The surprised man turned to her. The playful look on her face was taunting him. "I dare you."

"You think I won't do it?"

The undertaker polished off the rest of his drink and clapped his hands. Rhiannon watched in admiration, as he went swanning off across the hall. When he reached his destination, the young man knelt down before a gushing Liz Pugh and made his valiant request. Sure enough, Johnny had honoured his bet, and he was soon waltzing the birthday girl across the dance floor, much to the amusement of the crowd.

"He's not very in time with the music," said a bitter voice.

Rhiannon turned to see that a sticky looking Alun was now standing beside her, his white shirt now the close resemblance of a Jackson Pollock painting.

"Since when were you an expert?" she asked.

The moody accountant folded his arms. "I watch *Strictly*."

"You think you can do better?"

Alun's heart began to race. He could see that she was quite serious.

"Uh, well, I'm not —"

She grabbed his arm and pulled him towards the centre of

the room. "Come on, Anton Du Beke!"

Before he could work out where he was, the accountant was being swung around like a helpless puppet. Taking the lead and forcing him into an awkward jive, Rhiannon twirled her reluctant dance partner until he was dizzier than a cat on a merry-go-round.

Trapped in the woman's firm grip, Alun glanced up to see her making eye contact with a passing Johnny, who was still very much engaged with his own partner. In an effort to distract their nauseating exchange, the accountant suddenly began to replicate the elaborate steps of a young Fred Astaire. This unexpected display of dance moves caught his partner by surprise, and instead of impressing the woman with his knowledge of a dated tap dancing routine, he sent her flying to the floor with an awkward trip.

The laughter that followed was enough to end Alun's interest in dance forever. Rhiannon, on the other hand, had found his ballroom blunder rather amusing, and she willingly accepted the offer of a helping hand from her saviour Johnny Roberts.

The room prepared to shift its attention back to more pressing matters (like the abundance of free food and drink), only to be interrupted by the *clinking* of a wine glass. All eyes were now on a late arrival who was standing in the open doorway, a person who many had assumed was not invited. The hall was struck by a stone cold silence, as it appeared the music system's power chord had been mysteriously unplugged.

"Can I have everyone's attention, please!" said a slurring Gwen Tudor, tapping her spoon against an empty wine glass.

"What is she doing here?" hissed a furious Liz Pugh.

The drunken receptionist unleashed a wicked grin. "I would like to take this opportunity to make a speech..."

The stunned hotel manager was suddenly overcome by an appropriate feeling of sheer dread.

CHAPTER 17

"I would like to take this opportunity to celebrate the life of my dearest Auntie Lizzie..."

The words of Gwen Tudor echoed out across the hall. Although they should have been received as a gesture of kindness, Liz Pugh trembled in her colourful dress, dreading what she was about to say next.

"Most of you know Lizzie as your illustrious leader," Gwen continued. "But there is a lot more to Lizzie than her role in this hotel..." Her words slurred as she spoke, like a person who had been having her own little party for most of the afternoon. "Why don't you come up here and join me, Auntie?"

The young woman turned around, grabbed a fresh bottle of wine and began pouring it into her glass.

"I think you might have had enough of that, love."

She turned to find a concerned looking gardener in his favourite (and only) shirt.

"Ah, Robin," said Gwen. "The loyal gardener! Now, if anyone knows our family, it's you."

The man tried to take the bottle from her hand but failed,

miserably. "Don't you go saying things you might regret tomorrow."

"Like my mother, you mean? She's always been good at keeping quiet. Everything I want to say needs to be heard!"

"Stop making a fool of yourself, girl!" a voice croaked from the other side of the hall.

Gwen's eyes lit up at the sight of Angela Pugh stewing in her chair. "What a surprise to see you, Granny! If it's not the wicked stepmother who barged her way in!"

"How dare you!" Liz roared. "That's your grandmother!"

Her niece giggled and stumbled over towards the centre of the floor. "Mmmm... she's not really, though, is she?"

"She's the wife of your grandfather — and *my* father!"

"Ah, now that's where things get interesting," said Gwen, honing in on her aunt like a predator closing in on its helpless prey. She saw the horror in Liz's eyes. "Oh, wait... Nobody else here knows our little family secret, do they?"

"Gwen!" Angela croaked out.

The entire room waited in anticipation. The staff felt very little sympathy for these two family members, but they were revelling in the unexpected drama.

The young woman turned to her audience and prepared to put them all out of their misery: "You see, everyone, your beloved manager, Liz Pugh, is not a real Pugh at all!" Sensing that her aunt was on the verge of an explosion, Gwen decided it was probably safer to move herself away. "Unlike my mother, Rowena — the one and *only* daughter of the late Sir Dylan Pugh — Lizzie here, is the result of a scandalous affair!"

Rhiannon watched this airing of dirty laundry with great intrigue. A juicy scandal was a reporter's best friend, even if only a handful of people really cared. She was glad to see that the young woman was still alive and well, although what had ever possessed her to return to the *Balamon Hotel* she would never understand.

"Yeah, that's right," Gwen continued, reaching out her arms like a magician on her final reveal. "The *real* heir to this estate is living quietly in a semi-detached bungalow, whilst her so-called sister and wicked stepmother takes everything — like Cinderella without the pumpkin!"

Liz had heard enough. She abandoned all sense of social protocol and darted forwards to grab hold of her outspoken gate crasher.

"You ungrateful, little rat!" she cried. "My sister made her choice the moment she walked out of those doors. She didn't want anything to do with this place!"

"And you wonder why!" said Gwen, fighting back against those manicured hands, as they clasped her by the scruff of the neck.

"I think it's time to leave," said the gardener, planting himself between them before the teenager lost an eye.

Gwen took her opportunity to escape the clutches of her furious aunt and scooted back towards the drinks table. "Oh, but you haven't even heard the best bit!" She poured herself another drink and swallowed it whole. "I bet you're all dying to find out who the *real* father is!"

The room remained quiet. Their mouths said nothing, but their faces were crying out for her to spill the beans.

"He is a man you are all very familiar with," said Gwen. "A person most of you waited on hand and foot over the last few months."

"Oh, please no," Rhiannon muttered.

Alun was sharing the exact same thought process. If what they were both thinking was true, then everything was about to get a little more complicated.

"Lizzie Pugh's father," Gwen continued, "is none other than

the late, great — Mr Don Fletcher!"

Her audience gasped. They all turned to look at Liz, whose distraught face said it all.

Her niece was just about to pour another glass, when a firm hand grabbed her arm.

"Okay, I think that's enough," said Rhiannon, escorting her away from the drinks table with the urgency of a nightclub bouncer. "Let's get you some fresh air."

"Wait!" Gwen cried. "I haven't finished! There's still more!"

"I think you've said enough!" cried Angela Pugh, her cane waving in the air.

"How about we discuss the ending over a cup of cocoa," Rhiannon insisted.

Gwen's cries of protest were ignored, and soon she was dragged out of the room by the determined older woman. When the door finally slammed shut behind them, a shell-shocked Liz Pugh turned to her guests with an apologetic smile.

"So sorry about all that," she said. "Shall we have some cake?"

On the other side of the wall, Rhiannon was still walking her stumbling drunk towards the safety of the lobby. Gwen's previously excitable mood had already descended into a fog of depressed confusion.

"I was just about to expose Don's killer," she groaned. "Right in front of everybody!"

"Is that really a good idea?" Rhiannon asked.

"I'm not afraid of anything anymore! I refuse to be the victim. My mother's quite happy to run away, but I'm not letting people get away with anything! Not anymore!"

"I can see that. But most people would think about going to the police first."

Gwen dug her heels into the ground and yanked herself away. "Yes!" she hissed. "They would! Just like you did!"

"I didn't —"

"You told them about the death threats! After you promised me you wouldn't!"

Rhiannon sighed in defeat. She hadn't planned to have this conversation quite just yet, but it seemed the young woman had left her no choice.

"Gwen, was it you who broke into Angela's room that morning? Is that why you couldn't go to the police?"

The two questions almost sobered the young woman back up, at least, for a moment. She took her time with the answer: "I was taking back what is rightfully my mam's." The red mist descended again. "She received *nothing* when my grandfather died. It all went to that barking old woman, and as soon as she's carked it, Liz will get everything. It's not right!"

Rhiannon saw the hatred in the young woman's eyes. It was the same hatred that could drive a person to commit the unthinkable, and instead it seemed as though it was Gwen's life who was at risk.

The journalist found her humanity for a moment (something she did still have but that she would never admit it) and placed a caring hand on the younger woman's shoulder.

"Is the person you saw leaving Don's room in that very dining hall?" she asked finally.

Gwen's sharpness had been dulled many drinks ago, but there was still a glimmer of her true self coming back through.

She nodded in answer to the question.

The journalist held her close. "Who? Who was it, Gwen?"

"There you are!" said a voice from behind.

They turned to see Carys Roden making her way down the hallway. The assistant manager fumbled over her long dress, which seemed to have been more appropriate for a nineteen-twenties wedding.

"We need to find you a room," she said. "I had no idea you were coming."

Her words didn't appear to be registering with the woman whose face had now become grey with nausea. A groggy Gwen swayed on the spot, until she vomited all over Rhiannon's favourite shoes.

"Maybe we should finish this conversation in the morning," said the journalist, as she saw Gwen was beyond the stage of stringing together a cohesive sentence and well on the way to passing out right in front of her.

"Let's find you a room," said Carys, heading towards the back of the reception desk.

Gwen had collapsed to her knees and began sobbing in her deliriously drunken state.

Back in the dining hall, the party had managed to salvage the rest of its evening with an impromptu *Grease* medley. Alun sipped on his vodka and coke, whilst being forced to watch a disastrous rendition of "You're the one that I want". Every whiff of flavour reminded him of his stained shirt, and he decided that it might have been a good time to retire to his room.

Liz Pugh was now stewing on her own in the corner, watching over her drunken guests, who seemed to be having a much better time than she was. She had tried not to let Gwen's unexpected outburst ruin her evening, but it seemed like the damage had already been done.

As the hours went by, the numbers slowly dwindled, until there were only a handful of partygoers left. Rhiannon had decided to join the group of stragglers, if only for the company. The loneliness of her hotel room had not been appealing, and, instead, she had opted to surround herself with strangers. Alun's early departure had come as a disappointment, but she was determined to try and make the best of it, especially with a few glasses of Prosecco down her.

"Cheer up," said Johnny, as he snuck behind her in an oversized floral bucket hat he had just pinched.

"I'm quite happy, actually," she replied.

"Your face says otherwise." He pulled an exaggerated frown which caused her to smirk.

"Well, you're not the first to point out that I have a resting frown face. That's just the way it looks."

"Well, I think it's very pretty."

He leaned in, until their noses were almost touching. Suddenly, his previous attractiveness began to fade away. His forward manner and the stench of booze on his breath was an enormous turn-off.

"Thanks," she said, backing away so he was out of reach. "You should tell my parents. It's all down to them."

"How about we ditch this lot and have a few drinks upstairs," said Johnny, his body following her as though they were bound by a magnetic field. "We could have our own little party."

"Nah, you're alright. I don't party very long these days. I prefer an audio book and a cup of tea."

She swallowed the rest of her glass and checked the time.

"Whatever rocks your boat," Johnny persisted, placing his hand against her waist.

She pushed his arm away. "I think I've been pretty direct."

Johnny laughed. "Your type always love playing hard to get. Fortunately, I don't take no for an answer..."

Rhiannon felt her body go tight, as he grabbed both of her wrists and forced her into a strange dance. Just as the man was going to attempt a kiss, his head was struck by a clenched fist.

A dazed Johnny stumbled backwards, the alcohol in his system disrupting his senses. Steadying his blurred vision, he saw another man standing there between them.

"She said no."

Rhiannon turned to find a riled-up Alun, who was clutching

his bruised fist as if it were about to fall off.

Johnny was about to retaliate, until he noticed that the entire room was now watching him. The sight of all those eyes caused him to put his next move on hold, at least for now, and rather than initiate a vicious beating, he decided to rub his bruise and laugh.

The accountant could not have been more relieved. He had not thought through his impulsive punch, and he had no contingency plan for the inevitable counter attack.

"And they say chivalry is dead!" Johnny cried. "Isn't that adorable!" The undertaker swanned over to the drinks table and grabbed himself an entire bottle of whiskey. "Well, I don't know about everyone else, but I'd say this party's taken a dive." He slapped Alun on the back and strolled towards the doorway. "I'm off to see if I can have some *real* fun!"

He left behind an atmosphere that was more akin to a saloon after last orders. The music continued to play but the dancing was nonexistent.

Alun let out a sigh of relief and felt someone grabbing hold of his wrist.

"It hurts, doesn't it?" Rhiannon asked.

Alun's lower lip swallowed the one above. "It *really* does."

"Come on. There's an ice bucket in my room."

She dragged him out of the hall to the sound of Fleetwood Mac's "Seven Wonders".

A drunken Gethin shook his head as he reflected on the night's events. "What a party..." the concierge muttered.

Over on the outside of the building, Johnny Roberts was lighting up a cigarette and enjoying the cool, nighttime air. He heard a jingle from his phone and pulled it out to read the text message: *Room 28.* His eyes lit up, as he realised it was from Gwen. After a final exhale of smoke, he swigged his bottle of whiskey and headed back inside.

CHAPTER 18

Carys Roden's scream was loud enough to wake up the entire second floor.

Johnny Roberts groaned, as he opened his eyes to the flash of daylight coming in from the hotel room window. He could feel that the woman in the bed next to him was limp, and he saw that the white bedsheets were stained in a colour that would alarm anyone who had just woken up. To his great surprise, Gwen had not been disturbed up by the loud cry, and it appeared that she would not be waking up ever again.

The sight of the trembling assistant manager in the doorway, and the appearance of an unfamiliar hammer near his hand, did not bode well. He knew at that very moment that he was in a lot of trouble. A lot of trouble indeed.

Five doors down, in room number twenty-three, a confused Alun Hughes was also waking up. Lying on the floor, with little more than a single pillow and a small sheet to keep him comfortable, the accountant saw Rhiannon's face poking into view from up above.

"Did you hear that?" she asked, before leaping out of bed and throwing on a dressing gown.

Alun dragged himself up from the floor. His back was in more agony than his swollen hand. It had been kind of Rhiannon to nurse his fist, but he would have much preferred a proper bed for the night. Being a gentleman was rather inconvenient when you had a bad back.

By the time he had joined her in the hallway, the entire floor had opened their doors. Hangovers were at an all time high and were not helping to ease the commotion that was now rocketing among the off-duty staff members. Liz had taken the liberty of providing anyone who did not live in the staff accommodation next door a free room for the night, and they were now paying a hefty price with the wake-up call from hell.

Carys was still standing in the doorway of room number twenty-eight, her body frozen from the shock. "Someone call an ambulance!" the assistant manager screamed.

Panic followed, as every gawking spectator scrambled in search of their phones. Rhiannon went running down the corridor, pushing each and every motionless bystander out of the way. She knew a minimal amount of first aid and had decided someone needed to do something other than just nothing at all.

When she finally entered the room, the sight she found was enough to make her highly regret the decision, and it was clearly too late for any form of first aid. Johnny was lying over Gwen's motionless body, searching in desperation for a pulse. He had seen enough bodies in his profession to know when all hope was lost. After a final check of the neck, the undertaker looked up at the horrified journalist with a grave expression. He swallowed hard and prepared to utter a word that was quite common in his line of work: "She's... *dead*."

THE POLICE HAD DESCENDED upon the *Balamon Hotel* like a hoard of ghostly reapers emerging from the shadows. There had not been such a grisly death in this part of Anglesey for quite some time — let alone a murder.

Officer Gwent had been the first on the scene, and the opportunity to call in the entire circus of crime scene specialists had given him a thrill he didn't often come by.

He stood in the hotel room, twirling his moustache, whilst observing the team of forensics hard at work with their photographing, dusting and scraping. He tried to imagine the initials DCI in front of his name. It certainly had a nice ring to it, he thought. Instead, the privilege went to the man in the corner with receding hair and a creased shirt.

"Officer Gwent!" the detective called, not for the first time.

The policeman shook himself out of the daydream and acknowledged the man from out of town. "Uh, yes — Sir."

"Has everyone been told to stay in the building until they've been released?"

Gwent had to think for a moment. "Of course! Most of them are staff members."

"The guests are all staff?" DCI Neale asked.

"A lot of them," said the police officer. "They were all staying over."

The detective sighed and didn't try to understand. There would be plenty of time for that later.

Further down the hall, in room twenty-three, Alun was still trying to console a restless Rhiannon, who was pacing up and down like a nervous Grenadier Guard.

"There's nothing you could have done," he said.

"It just doesn't make any sense," said Rhiannon. "Why would he do it? Why batter someone to death and then sleep next to her?"

Alun thought he would have enjoyed the sight of Johnny

Roberts being handcuffed and escorted away by the police. But even he had felt troubled by the whole scene, particularly as his younger brother had to watch. "People do strange things."

"Don't tell me you think he did it?" She had stopped marching now and was waiting for his honest opinion.

"I can't say I like the man," he said. "But it does strike me as a very strange thing to do."

His friend let out a sigh of relief. "Thank you!"

"One thing we can be sure about though: someone in this hotel had already threatened to kill her. Last night was the perfect opportunity."

"Exactly!" Rhiannon cried. "There were plenty of people who could have easily got their hands on a room key. All they had to do was sneak in during the middle of the night with that hammer. Gwen and Johnny were both heavily drunk." She paused and thought about her conversation with the young woman in the foyer. "And there was something else... She told me she was about to expose Don's killer."

"The person she saw leaving his room?"

"She said that they were at the party."

Alun looked into her panicked eyes. She was now directly in front of him. "Your hands," he said. "They're still shaking."

The journalist hid them behind her back and tried to shrug it off. "It's probably the hangover."

"You're still in shock. It's very common after finding a body. You should probably lie down."

"I'm fine," she insisted and headed to grab herself a drink of water.

The long silence that followed caused Alun to begin thinking about Rhod. He knew that the teenager and his brother lived alone, making Johnny the only guardian he had, as far as he knew.

He pulled out his phone and searched for the number that

the young man had given him at the harbour. After typing out the words: *where are you now?* (Rhiannon had been making sure that he stopped typing out lengthy text messages, particularly the ones that were more suited to a formal letter), he received the response: *Room 14*.

"I'll be right back," he said.

The hallway outside was still busy with impatient party guests, many of them itching to get away. Alun recognised a distressed looking Robin, who almost knocked into him as they crossed each other.

"Is everything alright?" he asked the gardener.

"Oh, dear, dear," muttered Robin, shaking his head. "They just called me in for an interview. God, I wish I'd never left it out."

"Excuse me?"

"It was only my bleeding hammer, wasn't it? I used it to help fix up a floorboard yesterday. I should never have left it on the reception counter! So stupid!"

He pulled out a handkerchief and began blowing out his large nose before wiping down some excess sweat from his forehead.

"I'm sure you never intended any of this to happen," said Alun, watching in horror as the hanky was slipped back into the man's pocket.

"Heavens, no! It's knocked us all for six, this has. Nothing like this has ever happened here."

Alun would have liked to agree with the man, but he knew that strange deaths were more commonplace at the Balamon than he would have thought. He bid the gardener a farewell and continued on his way in search of Room Fourteen.

He found Rhod standing by the window when he entered the correct room. The teenager looked out towards the gathering of police vehicles, his face gloomier than the overcast sky.

"Here you are," said Alun. "I was beginning to worry that you'd already gone home."

"Not much point," said Rhod. "There's nobody there."

"Oh, I suppose you're right." The older man tried to think of something appropriate to say. "I'm sorry, Rhod. About your brother."

"It's not your fault," said Rhod, his voice empty. "My brother's used to getting himself into trouble with the police. He was a nightmare when he was my age. My mam and dad used to go bonkers."

"I think this might be a little more serious this time, Rhod."

The teenager nodded. He knew full well that his brother's unfortunate placement next to a dead body and a murder weapon did not bode well for him.

"You don't think he did it, do you?" Alun asked.

"My brother's done a lot of stupid things. But there's no way he did this."

The accountant nodded and joined him at the window. It struck him that the police vehicles looked very out of place among these ancient surroundings. What was normally a peaceful garden was now overwhelmed by a frenzy of people in uniform.

"We'll get to the bottom of all this," he said, eventually. "I promise."

Rhod looked up to see the man's serious expression. He nodded in appreciation.

"If you need some help from the dead, just let me know."

Alun smiled and nodded back. "Well, we could start with going over what we know for certain," he said, walking over to the small table in the corner of the room and lifting up a pad of plain paper. "If there's anything I've learned from accounting, it's that you're better off starting with the hard facts."

The pen in his hand began to scribble out a floor plan that resembled a long corridor with a series of doors on either side.

"Gwen was found dead in this room here," Alun said, marking off a square near the top of the page. "She was brought here by the assistant manager at around nine o'clock last night." The pen wrote out the name *Carys* on a separate sheet of paper. If there was one thing Alun was good at (apart from accounting and floor plans), it was names. Labels were an important tool in his mind, whether that was for ledgers, objects or, in this case, living human beings. Everything needed to be organised, and to be organised, you needed a label. He had always hoped that his memory for names would have served him well in his social life, but, sadly, this had never been the case.

"At some point," he continued, "Your brother would have made his way into Gwen's room." He drew a line up his paper hallway. "How? Well, he would need a key, meaning the police would have found one in the room. Or…"

"He was invited in," said Rhod.

"Exactly."

"Johnny and Gwen have been sleeping together for a while."

Alun turned to him with a raised eyebrow.

"My brother is pretty vocal about his love affairs," Rhod added. "He's always boasting. Don't know why he thinks I'd be interested."

"Which explains why they were in bed together," said Alun, ticking off another box in his mind. "But it does not explain why he would then kill her."

He looked down at the floor plan. "We need to start by getting the occupants of every room in this hotel — on every floor. I'm sure the police will do the same."

"There's also some staff accommodation outside."

"There is?"

"It's a house-share. They pay the rent out of their wages."

Alun scratched his head. "Sounds like this is going to be harder than I thought."

"Johnny was supposed to be sleeping in this room with me," said Rhod, writing down his own name beside the number fourteen. He looked over at the separate twin beds. "But I guess it wasn't cosy enough."

Alun made another amendment and scribbled out two new names, this time beside door number twenty-three.

"Looks like Johnny wasn't the only busy one last night..."

Alun turned to see the teenager's look of admiration at the two names against one room: Alun and Rhiannon.

"Oh, it's nothing like that," Alun insisted with a blush.

Rhod gave him a cheeky wink of understanding. He'd heard it all before.

CHAPTER 19

The murder of Gwen Tudor had created quite a stir among the residents of Tremor.

People knew very little about her mother, Rowena, other than she was an estranged member of the wealthy Pugh family. The residents of the local community had very little need for a hotel such as the Balamon, but they certainly wouldn't be recommending the place. They had already heard plenty about the ghostly inhabitants, lurking among those ancient walls, which was only made more famous by the recent visit of a certain world-renowned medium.

One member of Tremor's population who was particularly interested in the murder (mainly due to the fact that her nephew was now the key suspect), was Leslie Roberts. When her other nephew, Rhod, came skulking up the garden path, she was already at the front door.

"Well, well..." she said, her look of disapproval in full force. "He's really done it this time."

Rhod hesitated in his approach. He knew his aunt was going to take great pleasure in the whole affair, and as his new legal guardian, the woman was going to offer him very little sympathy.

Leslie had only ever had nothing but disdain for her deteriorating brother, let alone his troublesome offspring.

"I want no trouble from you now," she added. "There'll be none of your *Goth* nonsense under *my* roof."

Rhod looked back at her permanent scowl and saw his future looking very bleak indeed. Life with his older brother had hardly been a walk in the park, but the prospect of getting through the rest of his teenage years with *this* woman was a disturbing one.

She showed him to his new room, a place that she insisted he remained at all times whilst he was living in her house. That suited the teenager just fine. As he lay in bed that night, his mind wondered to the thought of his brother. The man was probably lying on his own mattress at that moment, only a much harder one (and, perhaps, slightly cleaner than his auntie's spare).

He also thought about the name on the invoice he had found on the kitchen table, along with the retired teacher they had recently buried.

Had it all been a coincidence? Or was there a reason that business had recently started picking up?

He would need to dig deeper. As his accountant friend had told him: start with the facts. Even if his brother was indeed innocent, there were still plenty of unanswered questions, some he might not have wanted the answers to.

∼

ALUN STARED at his roast dinner as though he needed a magnifying glass.

"What's the matter?" Rhiannon asked, tucking into her soup and bread.

"This isn't what I ordered," replied Alun, almost heartbroken.

They both inspected his tiny portion of carefully stacked vegetables with a slither of beef on top.

"It's the roast beef," said Rhiannon. She tried not to smile.

"But... where's the..."

"Have you never had fine dining before?"

Alun picked up his cutlery and prepared to attempt a bite.

"Personally," Rhiannon continued. "I always go with the soup in a place like this. You can only go so wrong, and there's always the bread."

The accountant had never been very adventurous when it came to his food. He liked familiarity in all walks of life, including on his plate.

"I just feel sorry for the chef," he said, looking around at the quiet dining hall. "Their talents are probably wasted on this place."

They ate in silence for a moment, something that the pair had grown quite comfortable with. However, their peaceful meal was not to last for very long.

"There you both are!" said the voice of Liz Pugh. The woman scurried over to their table with complete disregard for any privacy. "What a day we're having. I really do hope all that business upstairs isn't ruining your stay with us."

"You mean the dead body in room twenty-eight?" Rhiannon asked, causing her dining partner to almost choke on his rare beef. "Nah. Can't let something like that spoil your visit, can you?"

The hotel manager studied her expression for a moment, trying to work out whether she was serious.

"Oh, good," she said, eventually. "I'm very glad. It's not something that happens here very often."

"Dead bodies? Or murders?"

"Uh, well, neither. It's all been a bit much. Those police officers have no consideration for the fact that you're trying to run a business."

"How selfish of them."

"Yes, quite. But I'm sure we'll get back to normal very soon. I can't be doing with anymore of their incessant questions."

Alun and Rhiannon had also had their fair share of questions that day. DCI Neale had been very curious about why an accountant and a journalist were up in a remote part of the country on a supposed "business trip". He was also particularly interested in their encounter with the deceased only a day before. Had Alun not made the effort to disclose the sauna incident to the police already, it would have not looked good (something he had made quite clear to Rhiannon).

"I'm sure they're just trying to get to the bottom of it all," he said to Liz, who decided to back track on her previous comment.

"Oh, yes — of course! It's all dreadful. Poor girl. I mean, she could be a right handful, as you probably saw, but nobody deserves to be murdered in their sleep. Still, the hotel must continue to operate." She looked back at their judgemental stares and checked her watch. "Now, enjoy the rest of your meal!"

The woman disappeared quicker than she had arrived.

"God, I can't stand that woman," Rhiannon said, keeping her voice down.

Alun nodded whilst chewing on his crunchy vegetables. "I'm sure you're not the only one."

"Still can't believe Don's her father."

"Well you didn't really know Don, to be fair. We never met the man."

"No, but you know what I mean. It's all very odd, isn't it? That gravedigger of a woman upstairs having an affair with a psychic guest. Right underneath her husband's nose? Didn't see that one coming when I met her. I thought she was a right boring old frog."

"Don was quite a *wealthy* psychic too, apparently," Alun added.

Rhiannon scrunched up her nose like a disgusted rabbit. "Sounds like Madam Lizzie's done alright for herself: a hotel from her mother on the way and now the inheritance of a wealthy... well... whatever that ghost-hugging man was."

"That's if Don's inheritance has definitely gone to *her*."

"Well, why wouldn't it? Beneficiaries are confidential, so it's not like we have any way of knowing."

Alun sat back in his chair and stared up at the ceiling decoration. His mind whirled, just like the circular patterns stretching out above him. "I'm convinced that the only way to find Gwen's killer is by working out what happened to Don."

"Well good luck with that. Surely it's harder to solve a murder where the only witness is now dead."

"We also need a motive."

"At least we know for sure why someone wanted to kill Gwen."

"Do we?"

Rhiannon looked up from her Beef Wellington. She knew that stare and it was one she hated. "Oh, here we go. Let me guess —- we can't assume or we risk missing the real solution, right? Like your precious accounting anomalies..."

Alun smiled back at her. He was almost proud. "Exactly."

The journalist rolled her eyes and continued with her meal. "Well, in my line of work, you don't get to the bottom of anything by sitting around pondering. You only get closer by actually speaking to people. Something you number crunchers seem to hate."

"We're lucky you have no trouble with the speaking part."

The sound of her knife and fork crashing against the plate made him jump. He couldn't help the remark but it didn't stop him from being nervous.

"Alun Hughes," said Rhiannon. "Did you just attempt a bit of light banter?"

Her playful smile gave him an unusual sensation, one he deduced might well have been a form of affection.

"Of course," he replied. "It was just banter. No truth to it at all."

She pointed her fork at him as though he was a piece of pastry on her plate. "You be careful, Alun Hughes. This cheeky new side to you might get you poked in the eye."

They enjoyed another comfortable silence, until the accountant decided to get something off his chest: "Oh, I hope you don't mind... but I booked myself a room here for a couple of nights."

Rhiannon seemed more surprised than he had expected. "The prospect of murder in a hotel a good selling point for you, is it?"

"Well, that's sort of why I decided to book it." She raised an eyebrow and waited for him to elaborate. "I thought, if both of us stay here, it might be better. You know, with it being a little... *dangerous.*"

He watched her clap with delight (again, not quite the reaction he had expected).

"So you thought you'd be my big, tough protector?" she asked, flexing her muscles like an Olympian. "That's very sweet. But I don't think it helped Gwen very much. And she had someone sleeping next to her."

She had him there, he thought. Whoever had snuck into room

twenty-eight the night before had succeeded without detection. Alun was just as likely to receive a bump on the head as much as the next person — a disturbing thought if ever there was one.

"Are you sure you've not just had enough of Glenda's soap marathons?" Rhiannon asked. "She'll be heartbroken."

The thought of not going back to his bed and breakfast bungalow in Tremor was certainly an added bonus to the accommodation switch, but Alun had decided he was going to keep that little detail to himself.

"It's got nothing to do with my bed and breakfast," he said in a tone that he hoped might convince her.

"Welcome aboard the madhouse then, me hearty." She raised her wine glass for a toast. "How about we have another look at your map."

After a clink of their glasses, they both studied the hand-drawn floor plan, and Alun noted down a few more names beside each door from a slip of paper.

"I spoke to Carys earlier," he said. "I managed to get a rundown of the other people staying on the second floor. She told me that this room was hers — the one next door to Gwen's — which makes sense why she chose that one for her. She must have known it was already vacant."

The journalist watched him write down a handful of new names: Gary, Siwan, Gethin, Elgan.

"Who's this person in the room opposite Gwen's?" Rhiannon asked, pointing to the door on the opposite side of the hallway. The name beside it read: *Mark*.

"He's the chef apparently," said Alun.

They both looked down at their meals; Alun's was barely touched whilst Rhiannon's was already wiping up the last of her sauce.

"Maybe it's time we offered our compliments," she said.

"I can hardly wait."

The kitchen was only a closed door away and was surprisingly modern for such an old building. Its stainless steel surfaces gleamed in the harsh lighting and there appeared to be only a single member of the team on duty: a young sous chef called Rhys.

"Who said you could come back here?" he asked, chopping up a line of peppers beside a row of containers.

"I didn't realise we need authorisation," said Rhiannon. "It's a kitchen — not a secret lab."

The weedy young man, barely out of his teens, straightened himself up as if it was going to double his size. "Nobody is allowed in here without the proper uniform!"

"Says who?" asked his more confident intruder, who was poking her nose in one of the giant fridges.

"The head chef! It's healthy and safety regulations." Rhys dropped his chopping knife and began to stutter: "Heh — hey! You can't touch anything, either!"

Rhiannon closed the fridge and took another look around the immaculate kitchen.

"Well," she said, "I don't know who this very important chef is, but he's very lucky to have you standing guard. Where is this great man, then? Mark, is it?"

The sous chef froze, as he realised this woman was not going to be intimidated by the health and safety regulations, let alone himself.

"He's out the back," said Rhys. "He doesn't want to be disturbed." He watched her gaze at the small door. "Hey — no! You can't go back there!"

The junior chef's cries could be heard echoing in the distance, as Rhiannon and her side-kick strolled into a small courtyard outside. When they entered the enclosed space filled with piles of boxes and a handful of rubbish bins, the two were completely taken by surprise.

Instead of finding a chef on his cigarette break, they were presented with two unlikely lovers sharing a highly intimate moment. A startled Liz Pugh almost cried out in fright, whilst the man in her arms gasped with a face full of lipstick.

"Oh, hello, Liz," Rhiannon said, before acknowledging the man beside her. "Mark, I take it?"

CHAPTER 20

"I hope we're not interrupting," said Rhiannon, enjoying the hotel manager's embarrassment.

Liz Pugh darted away from the head chef as though he had suddenly burst into flames.

"Oh, uh — no, I was just..."

The woman straightened out her clothes and didn't even bother to finish her sentence. Her extremely close relationship with the head chef had been abruptly exposed, and she knew it was pointless to ignore it. It did not, however, make the whole moment any less awkward.

"This is not what it looks like," she added. "Mark and I have known each other for a very long time."

"You don't need to defend yourself," Rhiannon reassured her. "We're all flesh and blood here." She turned to Alun and found a gormless stare that reminded her of a naïve youth. "Well, some of us more than others."

Liz, who still seemed very hot and flustered, tried to shake her discomfort away and forced her voice back into its usual high-pitched tone. "Yes, well, anyway. I better keep moving — lots to do around here."

She bid them an awkward farewell and almost stumbled into a crate of bottles on her way out of the courtyard.

Unlike his manager, the chef seemed quite pleased with himself and lit up a cigarette.

"Who are you two, then?" he asked the two strangers. "Not more coppers looking for a chat, I hope."

His onlookers gave each other a confused glance.

"Uh, no," Rhiannon assured him. "I'm a reporter."

Mark scoffed. "Even worse! I wondered when you lot would come crawling out of the dirt. You journos aren't usually too far behind the old bill."

Alun coughed. "Actually I'm an accountant."

Rhiannon gave him a disapproving stare.

"Sounds like you're no stranger to a police investigation," she said. "Been involved in a few, have you?"

The chef scrunched up his brow and inhaled his cigarette. "I know my rights." He studied the unlikely pair with curious precision. "If you've come all this way for a story, you won't have much luck here. The place is a dead-end."

It was a poor choice of words, Rhiannon thought, but she suspected the chef wasn't the most sympathetic person in the world.

"I actually came to offer my compliments," she said. "The Beef Wellington was superb."

Mark chuckled. "Oh, yeah? Tell me something I don't know."

"How modest of you."

"I'm a chef," the man said. "There's no place for modesty when it comes to the kitchen. If your heart's not in it, then you shouldn't be cooking."

"I think we know where *your* heart lies," said Rhiannon.

Mark took a moment for her comment to sink in and then he smirked. "Oh, that? Yeah. Lizzie and I have always been close."

"There's close and then there's *close*. So what is it about her that first attracted you? The charming personality? The impeccable dress sense? Or was it the money?"

The amused chef almost choked on his cigarette. "Blimey, there's no beating about the bush with you, is there?" He shook his head and laughed again. "Money... *What* money?"

Rhiannon folded up her arms. "I think you know. Her mother only owns a great big castle. Then there's the inheritance from her biological father. I hear he was worth a few bob."

The chef took a deep inhalation of nicotine and puffed out a cloud of smoke. "That's right... You were at the party, weren't you? I thought I'd seen you before."

"How observant of you."

"Well, I know everyone in this place. I've been here long enough. New people stand out around these parts. Sounds like you enjoyed the display from young Gwen? She dished out a few bombshells in her little rant."

"You really didn't know about Don being Liz's father?"

"Unlike him, I'm not a psychic," said Mark "I don't think anybody knew — except Lizzie and her mother. They love a good family secret, that lot. It explains why the bloke was squatting here for so long. He even requested a DNA test, apparently." The chef paused to enjoy a cruel thought. "I bet old Angie was furious about that!"

He flicked away his cigarette butt and headed back inside as if his visitors were not even there. It was only once he had reached the middle of the kitchen that he realised the persistent journalist was still close by.

"You run a tight ship," Rhiannon said, admiring the neatly arranged selection of knives. "Whatever brought you to the *Balamon Hotel* in the first place?"

It wasn't like this when I got here," said the chef, grabbing hold of Rhys' latest vegetable container and chucking it back over the chopping board. "Do it again! Like I told you."

The nervous sous chef lifted up his knife and began decimating a new pile of chopped tomatoes with the vigour of a madman.

"That's more like it!" his boss cried, turning to his two guests. "That's how I turned this place around — it's all in the little details."

Alun tried to look impressed but he had never understood why people got so excited about a bolognese sauce. As long as it contained mince and tomatoes then he was happy.

"They must have been relieved to have you," he said. "I've not had food like that in any hotels I've stayed in."

He was sort of telling the truth: he had never eaten a meal so small, and he had only ever stayed in one hotel before (which was technically more of a guest house). Rhiannon had told him on a number of occasions that he really needed to get out of Pengower more. And there he was.

His attempt to stroke the head chef's ego had worked, and the man seemed to be more relaxed. He leaned back against the spotless counter surface and loosened his apron.

"I've worked all over," he said. "London, Paris, New York... you name it. But it's a young person's game, really. I've seen a lot of good chefs burn out over my career. You gotta get out whilst the fire's still burning."

"So you come to the edge of an island?" asked Rhiannon.

"That's most people's dream, isn't it? Living out the rest of your days on an island by the sea."

The journalist could not think of a worse existence than wasting away on a sunbed. She had never been the holiday type, and she doubted her distaste for lying in the sun would ever change. Give her a red-hot assignment with an element of danger and she was as happy as Larry. "Tremor is hardly the Caribbean," she said.

"It might as well have been when the job came up," said the

chef. "I remember the advert like it was yesterday. I was at the end of my third failed marriage and there it was in the back of my newspaper: *Rural, Welsh hotel in need of chef. Accommodation provided.* Sounded alright to me."

"So you live here, at the hotel?" asked Alun. He had already heard about the nearby staff accommodation, and it seemed as though there might have been more occupants in there than he would have first thought.

"Have done for over ten years," Mark said, proudly. "Free accommodation and my very own kitchen — I feel like the luckiest chef in the world."

"How many of you are living in that house?" the accountant asked again. "I presume it's the house next door we're talking about."

"There's a few of us in there. People have come and gone over the years but there's plenty of room. The building's massive. I think it used to be a manor house or something."

Rhiannon picked up one of the sharp knives and began inspecting the razor-sharp blade with a strange fascination. It was making the two men in the same room as her a little uncomfortable and she enjoyed that. There was nothing like a knife to get people's attention.

"So there's a lot of invested staff members in this place," she said. "If someone were to lose their position at the Balamon, it could also mean losing a place to live. Am I right?"

Mark seemed more amused by her knife inspection than intimidated. "Are you implying that there's a reason people should be worried about their jobs?"

"There would be if someone were to decide to sell the place," Rhiannon replied.

"And where on earth did you hear that?" asked the chef, with a scoff. He looked over towards his sous chef, who up until this point had not really been listening. *Now* he was fully engaged.

"Nowhere in particular. I'm just presenting the possibility, that's all. Hotels change ownership all the time. Many close down altogether." She put down the knife and began moving in the direction of the curious man in his bright white uniform. "You'd be okay, though."

He stared her down, as she stepped closer. "*Would* I now?"

"Of course you would," Rhiannon continued. "Liz wouldn't let anything happen to you... her secret lover. You've been married once — why not again? There'd be a lot of money in it for you."

Mark turned to look at Alun and exposed a gold crown with his enormous laugh. "Is she always like this?"

Alun shrugged. "Mostly, yes."

"You can tell she's a writer," said the chef, before turning back to address his stern interrogator. "Quite the imagination you've got there, girl. But I'm afraid you've lost the plot on this one.

"Which one of you made the first move, then? Let me guess: you cooked her a nice dinner."

The man was starting to lose his sense of humour, and the smarmy grin had begun to fade. "Are you seriously insinuating that I've seduced a wealthy woman into sharing all her money?" He grabbed a handful of his belly fat and shook it. "Sorry, love, but I'm not the seductive type."

"True love, then, is it?"

Rhiannon was now right up in his disgruntled face. She could smell the cooking oil emanating from his large pores.

"It's a bit of fun," he said, firmly. "Nothing more than that. So why don't you take your little, judgemental journo hat and sod off out of my kitchen."

The woman held her stare and let out half a smile. She knew that his smug demeanour had to break eventually, and she had been waiting to wipe that arrogant smirk off his face.

Alun gave her the signal: it was time to leave. Rhiannon reluctantly conceded, and she gave the man back his personal space.

"Oh, I almost forgot," she added, "that pastry was absolutely divine!"

They both left the head chef and his apprentice to their chopped vegetables and made their way back into the dining hall.

"There was no need for all that," said Alun, as they returned to their table.

"Yes there was," said Rhiannon.

Her dinner date looked down at his unfinished meal. It was less appealing now than it had been when it was hot.

"You know they'll be spitting in your food from now on," he said. "It's why you should never complain when there's food involved. Chefs hold all the power."

Rhiannon looked back towards the kitchen door and snarled. "Well I think that chef's got his feet right under the table in this place. I don't trust him as far as I could throw his giant head."

She picked up the menu and gazed over its wide selection of puddings. Anything with chocolate was always the answer when it came to a bad mood, and she felt one coming on like an approaching freight train.

"Fancy ordering some desert?"

CHAPTER 21

The triple chocolate ganache had been three chocolates too many. Rhiannon lay on her bed with the biggest sugar coma known to man. Why she did it to herself was beyond her own understanding, and, yet, despite the increasing nausea that would probably ruin her upcoming sleep, she would have done it again in a heartbeat (it was, after all, the most delicious ganache she had ever tasted).

As she closed her eyes for an early night, the rumble on her bedside table made her jolt with fright. Flashing on her mobile phone screen was an unknown number. Unlike most people, the prospect of an unknown caller meant that she was far more likely to answer it than she was for a person she knew. It was either her antisocial nature or relentless curiosity as a journalist.

"Hello?" she asked, silencing the angry vibrations.

"I didn't think you were going to pick up," said the male voice.

Rhiannon sat up against her headboard. She recognised the voice and it was the last person she had ever expected.

"How did you get my number?"

The sound of the man's breath crackled in her ear. Johnny Roberts seemed to be enjoying making her wait.

"I got it from my brother's phone a couple of days ago," he said. "I thought it might come in handy if you were one of those women who prefers to take the *man's* number."

Rhiannon squeezed the phone in her hand. "I'm neither, actually."

The chuckle that followed made her tighten even more. "Clearly." A nasty cough followed. "Excuse me. I think I've got a cold coming on. They're treating me like an animal in here."

"I'll go fetch the violin," said Rhiannon.

"Don't worry, I'm not calling for sympathy."

"On that note — why are you calling me, exactly? You probably only get one call. Shame you've wasted it."

"I couldn't think of anyone else who could help me."

"Try a good solicitor. Or maybe your brother."

Johnny scoffed. "I'm going to need one hell of a solicitor. And as for Rhod, well... there's not much *he* can do. The poor sod can barely help himself."

"Well, then maybe you should think about someone other than yourself for a change and call him."

She heard the line rattle for a moment as if the receiver on the other end was being shaken.

"Everything I've ever done has been for my family!" Johnny growled. "It's not easy supporting two people with a father in care. I've worked my hands to the bone."

Rhiannon listened to his voice breaking. It was the first time she had ever sensed a glimmer of emotion from the man.

"Nobody in that village has ever cared about us," he continued. "We Roberts' have always been the black sheep — the grave diggers — the people who bury everyone else's loved ones." After a series of sniffles he took a moment to compose himself again. "I'm calling you because I've been wrongly arrested for the murder of Gwen Tudor."

"That's nice. But I'm not your jury."

Johnny's snivelling had switched within a matter of seconds. All of a sudden, he seemed back to his playful self. "Come on, don't be like that. I know you're a truth seeker. I've read your work."

The journalist rolled her eyes. "You read the *Merioneth Press*, do you?"

"I've done my homework. As soon as I first saw you in that graveyard I couldn't help myself. I became a little obsessed, actually."

Rhiannon felt a sickness in the pit of her stomach (and it wasn't the chocolate ganache). The thought of someone obsessing over her was not a pleasant one, particularly a man who she had turned down for a one-night-stand and was now facing a murder charge. She had done her own fair share of unhealthy digging in the past, but having a person pour over her work like a deranged psychopath made her very nervous indeed.

"I'm hanging up now," she said, eventually.

"Just promise me you'll have a look into it," Johnny pleaded.

"That's the police's job."

Another scoff crackled its way down the line. "The police don't care about proving my innocence! They've got everything they need for an easy case. They won't want to complicate things for themselves." His voice began to break again. "Think about how you'd feel letting an innocent man go down."

"My conscience is as clear as crystal."

"Please. Just — see if you can find some kind of evidence. That's all I'm asking."

Rhiannon hung up the phone and chucked it back on the bedside table. She lay back down against her pillow and stared up at the ceiling. After letting the nature of the call wash over her, she reached back across and switched off her phone.

On the other side of her bedroom wall, Alun was lying in his own bed, pouring over his copy of Don Fletcher's tattered paperback.

Although he had never met the late medium before his untimely death in the bathroom not too far from his own, he was getting a reasonable insight into the man's younger self. It seemed that Don's talents had not been restricted to merely an expertise of the departed, but he had also possessed a great deal of charm and eloquence.

Alun had remembered the first time he had come across a world-renowned hypnotist during a mindless flick through the channels of his television. The performer had captivated an entire studio audience and, with the power of his oozing charisma and undeniable stage presence, had wowed the impressionable young man with a feat of telekinetic wonder.

Many years later, the more cynical and practical Alun had deduced that such displays of supernatural abilities were nothing more than a parlour trick — something a confidence thief would use on a busy street.

It was only during his rekindling with the world of psychics and hypnotists that his older and more withered mind had started to become reopened to the idea. The prospect of speaking to a loved one beyond the grave had always been more tantalising than nightmarish. There had been so many conversations he had wished he'd had with both his mother and father whilst they were still around. If there was just the smallest chance that a human being was capable of even a brief exchange of words, then surely it was worth a try?

He placed the book down and looked around his new accommodation, which had been a vast improvement from his tiny space Glenda's spare room. The high ceilings freed his overactive mind, and he began thinking about the various ghostly inhabitants that supposedly wandered these vast rooms. As terrifying as it would have been if one of them suddenly presented themselves at the edge of his queen-sized bed, he strangely longed for the experience. Perhaps the appearance of a howling spectre was, in his own mind, a form of proof that the dead were still with us. And if *that* were true, then the possibilities were endless.

After ruminating on the idea of a brief interview with the ghost of Don Fletcher, something that would have been extremely useful under the circumstances, he reached for his mobile phone and searched the name *Rhod*.

Text messaging had never been his forte, and when he came to deciding what to write, he made sure to do what everyone else seemed to do — keep it short: *Hope everything is okay*. The sentence seemed short enough, although he could imagine the youth of today abbreviating such a general statement even more. It didn't quite have the elaboration of a phone call, or the personal touch of a letter, but he hoped it would be enough to show the young man that at least *someone* was concerned about him.

He scrolled through a series of what he had heard were referred to as "emojis" and thought that perhaps a small image might cheer the young man up. After debating between a closed fist and a face with glasses and a large row of teeth, he went with a simple thumbs up and decided to play it cool.

Soon the message was flying up into the ether, and the tired accountant decided to get himself some rest. A minute later, just as he was about to doze off, his phone let out a short *ding*. His eyes squinted at the bright glow, and he read the words: *Fine. U?*

Alun's heart sank. The thought of responding to a two-worded message gave him a headache. It seemed his brain was not cut out for this strange form of communication. Narrowing down your sentences to the vocabulary of a toddler was surprisingly difficult.

Once he had spent the next ten minutes deliberating his next message (and choice of emoji), he decided to abandon the task altogether and press the call button.

"It's only me."

"I knew it was you," said Rhod's voice. "Your name came up on my screen, remember? Plus you were just messaging me."

"Oh, I know that. It's just something I've always said. I think it's an old habit from using landlines."

The line went silent.

"I didn't wake you, did I?" Alun asked.

"Nah. I don't usually go to sleep until about two."

The older man tried to fathom the idea of such a late bedtime but decided it was best not to dwell on it too much.

"Did they find you somewhere to stay?"

"I'm living with my Auntie Leslie," said Rhod.

"Oh, that's good."

"Not really. She's the most vile woman I know."

"Oh. I see."

Another long pause followed. Alun was starting to regret making the call altogether, and although he only had the best intentions, he had never been very good at personal conversations, especially with an awkward teenager. He scratched his head a few times and then caught sight of Don Fletcher's face grinning back at him from the cover of his paperback.

"What do you know about physical mediumship?" he asked.

"What did you just say?"

"It's apparently a type of trance mediumship that involves —"

"I know what it means," Rhod interrupted. "I just didn't expect you to bring it up."

"Oh, well, you know... just making conversation, really."

"About trance mediumship?"

"It was either that or the weather. Just something that was on my mind."

Alun was beginning to wonder whether he had caused offence, until the voice on the other end of the phone cut off his next sentence with an unexpected lecture: "It's a process of manipulating energy systems. Physical mediumship specifically involves materialised spirit bodies."

The accountant allowed the burst of new information to wash over him. "Like a poltergeist?"

This time, the muted grunt signalled that he definitely had caused offence.

"It's a little more complicated than that," Rhod said, eventually. "You're thinking of a malicious spirit."

"Oh." Alun probably *was* thinking of malicious spirits. The clanking noises coming from his bathroom pipes had not helped with that. "There was mention of this trance mediumship stuff in Don's book."

"That's not surprising. Spirit operators were a huge part of Don's practices."

"Spirit —"

"Spirit operators. Spirits who use mediums to manipulate psychic energy. Hence why we're called *mediums*. We're like a vessel for energy."

"Like a conductor?"

"Uh, yes. I suppose so."

Alun nodded. *Now* they were talking his language. He could get his head around anything when it came to physics. Something was telling him that he was stumbling on a whole new world of knowledge, and it did not involve a single spirit operator.

"There are lots of different types of mediumships," Rhod continued. It was already the longest amount of time he had ever spoken to anyone else about his favourite subject (apart from Don, of course). "They all involve *channelling* to some degree, but in a different way. There's physical mediumship, like the manipulation of physical objects or sounds; trance mediumship, where the medium is conscious; mental mediumship, which is the most commonly recognised form. Mental mediumship uses an act of telepathy to pass on messages to the designated sitter."

"Like a mobile phone!" Alun said, almost too excitedly.

"Uh, yes. Sort of."

Now it was Rhod's turn to receive a silence. The man on the other end of the phone was still letting this information marinate in his curious mind.

"This, *mental* mediumship," he said. "Is that what people also refer to as a clairvoyance? Like a reading?"

"Are you trying to ask what I think you're trying to ask?" Rhod asked.

Alun smiled. It appeared the teenager was psychic after all. "I think I am. I've never done one, but I suppose it's never too late."

The line crackled, until Rhod's surprised voice came through again: "Alun, are you asking me to do a séance?"

CHAPTER 22

Rhiannon had not slept a wink since her strange call. It wasn't often that she was phoned up by someone looking for a favour, especially a person who had been arrested for murder. Normally, it was *her* doing the cold calling and rarely did they ever ring her back.

Instead of reliving the conversation over and over again in her sleepless mind, she decided to give the hotel bar a try.

Wrapped in a dressing gown that was two sizes too big, she strolled down the deserted hallway in her fluffy, pink slippers. As far as she was concerned, the Balamon was her temporary new home, and she might as well feel comfortable.

The old hotel seemed to possess a very different atmosphere during the quietness of the night. Its damp wallpaper and dusty carpets let off a musky smell that reminded Rhiannon of an old theatre she had once visited in London. Just like this building, it had suffered from decades of neglect and poor upkeep, to the point that it had felt as though it was slowly dying away.

She was not surprised about all the peculiar sightings that had supposedly been reported among these ancient walls. The dimly lit hallways and echoes of the howling wind outside were enough to play tricks on anyone's mind, including her own. With her senses heightened and her thoughts about Johnny Roberts still raw in her tired brain, the journey down the final staircase had come with a slight sense of relief.

An absence of people would normally be a welcome gift, but tonight, it had driven the woman to madness. She would have given anything to come across the sight of another guest or have a busy member of staff rush past her.

Unfortunately, the person she *did* come across was not someone she would necessarily have chosen.

"Are you alright Ms Williams?" asked the man greeting her at the reception desk. His tone had been with its usual air of forged concern.

"Yes, thanks," she replied. "Just fancied a nightcap."

The concierge looked her up and down with a disgust for her choice of clothing.

"Oh," said Gethin. "I assumed by your dressing gown and slippers that there had been an emergency."

"No," Rhiannon said defensively. "This is normally what I wear at this time of night. Like most people. Although I can't picture you in a pair of pyjamas. Do you even get undressed to shower?"

The man refused to indulge her and merely rolled his eyes. "Is there anything else I can help you with?"

The journalist looked over at the wall behind him. "Yes, there is, actually." She pointed at the rows of brass keys, all dangling in their correct places below a designated number. "Where were they stored last night?"

Gethin's hangover had reached its peak, and he appeared to be only hanging on by a thread. "Locked away in that cupboard."

The cupboard was more of a door, and it sat behind the counter with its stained panels.

"And who had access?"

The tired man sighed. "Listen, if you're trying to play detective, I've had enough of these sorts of questions for one day."

"So I take it you had a key." She watched him shudder.

"I didn't, actually. There are only two keys to that door, and one's a spare. The guest has one and a manager has the other."

Rhiannon nodded. It made perfect sense to her. But what didn't was the fact that someone else must have got hold of the spare key *that* night.

"So if Liz and Carys were the only ones who had access to the second key to Gwen's room, how would someone else manage to get in there?"

The concierge stared at her with a raised eyebrow. "Is that a rhetorical question?"

"Maybe. I'm not quite sure yet." The journalist stared off into the distance, her mind trying to work out all the various possibilities. This must have been what it was like to be stuck with Alun's brain, she thought. "Each room has a spare key, right?"

"Correct. Will there be anything else, madam?"

"So Gwen would have been given her own when Carys left her in the room and she had access to the other."

"Listen, if this is going to go on for a while —"

"And Carys would have used the second key the following morning when she found the body! So she was definitely the only other person who had the spare, meaning the killer had to have been let in somehow."

The concierge checked his watch. His heart sank at the thought of three more hours until the longest shift he had ever known was at an end.

"Listen," he said. "How about I save your little brain the trouble: Gwen Tudor's killer was the man lying in her bed next to that hammer. It doesn't take a world-class detective to work that one out."

"Ah, yes. The hammer..."

Gethin felt like he was going to pass out in front of her. His reception counter had become a cage for him to continue suffering long into the night.

"The hammer was behind the counter, wasn't it?" She didn't receive an answer. "God, if only there was CCTV."

"I'm starting to wish the hammer was still here."

Rhiannon froze. She saw the desperation in his face and decided to keep the rest of her thoughts to herself. "Well, there's no need to be rude," she said, before walking off and leaving the man in the bliss of his own company. She could hear his sigh of relief as she crossed into the next room.

The Balamon's small bar area was situated at the other side of the building and it featured a disused snooker table and an American-style jukebox that had stumbled straight out of the fifties.

Not surprisingly, the entire room was empty, except for the presence of a bored Mared reading through her magazine. The young woman slouched behind the bar like a sulking child who had been placed there against her will.

"It's rocking in here," Rhiannon said, as she entered the room in her flowing dressing gown.

"You can say that again!" said Mared, welcoming the opportunity to speak.

Her new customer pulled up a stool and joined her at the counter. "Aren't you normally housekeeping?"

Mared smirked. "I'm a bit of everything, me. They just fling me around the place like an old dishcloth. Tonight I get the pleasure of manning the bar." She raised up her arms and presented the empty room to her. "Talk about a graveyard shift. Nobody who stays in this place ever wants to have fun."

"Well, I'm about to make history." Rhiannon straightened herself up and pointed towards the row of spirit bottles. "I would like a Singapore Sling, please. And have one for yourself."

"Now we're talking!" Mared cried with an excited laugh. She flexed her finger joints and burst into life. Soon, the bottles were flying around like an old Tom Cruise film, until a loud *smash* caused her to pause. "Ooops."

They both stared down at the broken bottle of grenadine on the floor. "Or maybe just make it a gin and tonic."

The two women suddenly burst into laughter, as the embarrassed barmaid fetched her dustpan and brush.

Rhiannon hopped up and swanned over to the jukebox. "What do you fancy?" she called out.

"There might be some Taylor Swift on there if you're lucky!" Mared called back, scooping up the last of the shattered glass.

The older woman groaned out in protest. "*Now* you're showing our age gap. I expected you to have good taste."

A clink and a clank later, and the jukebox began blasting out its paying customer's selection. The musical intro to Ace of Base's "All that she wants" caused Mared to look up from her cocktail-shaking.

"Are you *serious*?" she asked. "It's not the eighties!"

Rhiannon was already swinging her hips in time to the saxophone solo. "This is nineties, actually!"

The disapproving bartender shook her head and slid a finished drink to the edge of the bar. "One Singapore Sling — no grenadine!"

Her satisfied customer nodded and strutted back to the bar like a boxer in a flamboyant robe. "Ta very much!"

The two clinked their glasses and enjoyed a burst of cherry and pineapple.

"I saw your little friend just now," Rhiannon said. "He was rotting away behind his counter."

The mere reference to the concierge soured the young

woman's drink. "He hates working reception. Luckily he doesn't have a choice, tonight — what with us being down a receptionist."

Rhiannon gazed up whilst she sipped on her straw. "You two didn't seem to be getting on very well at the party."

"That's because he's a conniving, little weasel," Mared muttered. "I hate the man with a passion."

"I mean, I can't see why anyone would like the bloke. But *hate's* a pretty strong word."

"That's because he's not got it in for you."

They took a moment to slurp through their ice-filled drinks.

"You seem alright to me," Rhiannon said. "Can't imagine why someone would ever take a disliking."

Mared added some extra suction to her straw and finished off the entire cocktail. Once her short brain freeze had subsided, she prepared herself for the response: "Some people don't like it when people aren't afraid to be who they really are."

Their jovial conversation had taken a heavy turn. Rhiannon raised her guard back up and waited for the woman to elaborate.

"Unlike *some* people," Mared continued, "I've always been quite comfortable with my sexuality. Out and proud! Always will be."

"He's homophobic? *That's* why he doesn't like you?"

"He doesn't like me, because I walked in on him kissing the Aussie trainer."

"You're kidding…"

Mared crushed a block of ice against her teeth and swallowed it. "The look on his face was priceless."

"So, Gethin's in a relationship with Billy?"

"He doesn't have the nerve. Gethin has barely spoken to the guy since. I've been sworn to secrecy about the whole thing. And as you can see, I'm not very good at secrets."

"Is it true about the drugs?" Rhiannon's question caused the other woman to frown. The assumption had clearly offended her. "Gethin mentioned on our first encounter that you supplied morphine to Don Fletcher."

Mared's mood lifted and her expression filled with mischief. "I thought you were talking about the weed. That snitch is still trying to get me caught on that one. Good job I've got some planted underneath his bed just in case. It's handy living with your archnemesis."

Rhiannon lifted up her head, which now had a beer mat stuck to it. "Gethin lives in the staff accommodation too? How many of you are there living here?"

The barmaid shrugged. "Quite a few. It's a good deal. The hotel doesn't have to pay us as much and we get free room and board. Everyone's a winner."

She grabbed their empty glasses and began preparing a second round. "This next one's on me."

"Can I ask you something?" Rhiannon asked, studying the array of tattoos around her forearms. "What even brought you to live here in the first place?"

"I was only supposed to be here a couple of months. Finished up with art college and saw a chance to make some easy cash." She handed her customer a finished cocktail. "I think I'm more curious to know what *you're* doing out here?"

Rhiannon picked up her straw and stirred. "Ah, well. That's a very long story."

"I've got a very long shift."

They both made a short toast and laughed.

"Well," said the journalist. "In a nutshell, I'm here because of a man who's not even alive anymore."

Mared nodded. "Don Fletcher."

"You sounded fairly close to the man — what with the morphine and everything."

"My cousin works at the chemist in Tremor. It's pretty easy

stuff to get hold of when you know how, but not if you're an elderly foreigner like Don. I quite liked the bloke from the start. I like anyone with a creative bone in them. He had this book he was writing about his life. I offered to proof it for him." The woman combed back her red hair and winked at her. "I'm a pretty harsh critic when I want to be. I think he liked that."

Rhiannon sat up straight and stared back at her with a newfound curiosity. "You read Don Fletcher's manuscript?"

Mared smiled. "Twice. And the man's got some pretty juicy stories about this place."

The journalist smiled back. "Well, like you said — you've got a very long shift. And I've got all night."

CHAPTER 23

The match ignited with a small flash. Alun watched the burning flame as it lit up a series of cheap candles that had been laid out in a circle. The lights had been switched off, and his hotel room now had the warm glow of a fading campfire.

Rhod extinguished the match and placed a plate of burnt sausages between him and the accountant.

"What are those for?" Alun asked, feeling slightly hungry after his tiny meal at the restaurant.

"Spirits still seek physical nourishment long after death," said Rhod, squirting out a blob of ketchup. "It can help lure them into the room."

"Sausages?"

The teenager sighed. "Yeah, it's not ideal. You normally want aromatic foods but this is all I could find left in the fridge. Plus they were Don's favourite evening snack."

"Fair enough." Alun watched the shadows dancing from the tiny flames. He hadn't realised it was so drafty. "Did you know about Liz being Don's daughter?"

Rhod began studying his small book of notes as though he

were preparing for an exam. "I knew that he had a daughter. He said he'd been trying to connect with her after all these years. I never would have guessed he was talking about Liz."

"This hotel is full of surprises," Alun said, readjusting himself on the hard floor. He had never been nimble, and the way his legs began falling asleep made him hope this wasn't going to take long. "We don't have to do this now, you know? I feel bad you coming all the way over."

Rhod shrugged. "I couldn't sleep in my auntie's room anyway. I'm allergic to cats and she has three. It was nice to get the fresh air."

The smell of the burning incense made Alun question his choice of the words: "fresh air". He was also starting to worry about the prospect of setting off the fire alarm.

"Have you ever done one of these before?" he asked, sensing the young man's nerves.

"Never," said Rhod (not filling the other man with much confidence). "But I've always wanted to. I've never known anyone I could try one with."

"Not even Don?"

The teenager shook his head. "We didn't need to. Don's psychic abilities were beyond the need for a séance. They're really designed to help non-clairvoyants have the chance to communicate."

How convenient, Alun thought. It probably saved the man on candle costs.

Rhod sat himself down on the floor so that both of them were facing each other. "This might get a little intense. You should really have at least three people in a circle but two will have to do."

He took hold of the other participant's hands and closed his eyes. The word "intense" had already caused Alun to gulp, and he was now beginning to regret the whole idea altogether. He had approached the notion of communicating with the dead quite cynically, but it didn't stop him from getting absolutely terrified.

Since his recent break-up with Megan, he had decided to make a lot more effort when trying new things, but perhaps the encouragement of paranormal activity was a step too far. Although he had never really believed in ghosts, or journeys beyond the afterlife, the whole idea of things going bump in the night filled him with terror. He hated horror films — particularly the ones with those cheap jump-scares — and God help the person trying to get him on a haunted house ride. The more he thought about it, the problem really resided in the possibility of being startled (whether that was by a howling face or an unexpected mouse). Ultimately, the accountant didn't like surprises. His whole profession was geared towards avoiding these things as much as possible. You could never be caught off guard if you anticipated problems in advance. And if there was one thing Alun hadn't preempted, it was that he would one day be sitting in a giant fire hazard with his eyes closed.

Rhod, on the other hand, seemed to be completely in the zone. His eyes were still closed, and after focusing on his breathing, he prepared to speak: "Our beloved Don, we bring you gifts from life into death. Communicate with us, Don, and move among us."

All that could be heard now were the rustling of trees in the wind outside. Both participants waited for a response, only to be met with a faint *creak* from the floorboards above them.

"What happens if we don't hear anything back?" Alun said, hoping they would have to stop.

Rhod ignored him and continued to stay focused. He repeated his previous two sentences, which in turn answered the other man's question.

After another period of silence, Alun jumped at the sound of a loud *clank* coming from the bathroom.

"What was that?" he cried.

The teenager urged him to relax, which at this point was nigh on impossible.

"I think it was the shower head again," Alun added. "It's been falling down since I got here. They really need to get it sorted."

Rhod hushed him and repeated his requests for a third time. Moments later, they heard a *knock*.

The accountant jumped again, this time even higher. "Was that the door? I think that was the door!"

Another *hush* followed from Rhod, who appeared to be trying to hear something.

"Someone's trying to say something," he said.

Alun's face went pale. "Is it Don?"

"No," replied Rhod, squinting his eyelids. "It's someone else."

He began tightening his grip and quivering his lips. All of a sudden, it was as if the teenager had been possessed by another being. Unfortunately for the accountant, it did not offer him much comfort and reminded him of a seventies horror film that he would have rather forgotten.

"The voice has an accent... a Welsh one."

It was not surprising, Alun thought. They were, after all, in the remains of a Welsh castle. There had probably been hundreds, if not thousands, of previous occupants over the centuries, but he wasn't keen on meeting any of them.

"He's telling me his name... Alun Hughes... but that's — that's *your* name!"

Alun felt his stomach go tight — even tighter than his grip on Rhod's fingers. Any hint of cynicism about what they were doing had faded away, and he felt a wave of emotion take hold of him. He knew who Rhod could hear. It was the same person he claimed to have seen by the harbour, the same person he had never expected to speak to ever again. And his eyes began to fill with a substance he hadn't felt since Megan left him.

"*Dad*?!" he cried out.

Rhod was concentrating hard, and he gave the man a gentle nod.

The third-generation accountant tried to hold himself together. He felt as though the walls around them had disappeared, and that they weren't in the hotel room at all. His mind had been transported to a different place, where his parents were still alive and he could speak to them whenever he pleased.

"What is he saying?" Alun asked.

"He says…" Rhod took a moment to decipher his message. "He says he's proud."

The other man's stomach tightened a few more notches, until his voice was a broken mess: "About the business?"

"No," said Rhod. "He's proud of *you*. As a son."

Alun wanted to cry out at the top of his lungs. His father had never been a very sentimental man, and he had certainly never used the word "proud". For all he knew, this strange teenager with the dark clothes and blue hair was completely having him on. But for that brief moment in time, he was willing to let go of his natural scepticism — he was willing to believe everything.

He would have given anything for the chance to be heard back, and as if by an otherworldly force, he began crying out in a delirious mess: "Dad!! It's me — Alun! Can you hear me?"

As would be expected, there was no response. Suddenly, Rhod looked even more uncomfortable than he already was.

"Are you alright?" Alun asked, who had seen someone suffer less with a bout of food poisoning.

"He's trying to warn us of something," the teenager said. "Something dangerous."

"Like what?!"

Rhod groaned, and before he had a chance to answer, their hands were pulled apart. In the time it would have taken to turn on the lights, the intensity of this strange ceremony was over. Alun sat himself back and watched the young man breathing heavily, like a cat that had been rescued from a fish pond.

The room had returned to its tranquil state, and everything that had just happened almost seemed a little silly.

"What was he trying to warn us about?" Alun asked again.

Rhod finished catching his breath and shook his head. "I'm sorry, I couldn't make it out. I don't have the stamina."

Alun struggled to hide his disappointment. "Well, I suppose it's not something a person does everyday."

They sat in silence for a while, as the tiny candles melted into their pools of clear liquid.

"No sign of Don, then?" Alun asked. He spoke as if channelling the dead was just a brand new application on his mobile phone. It was surprising how quickly a person could get used to discussing such a subject. Perhaps it was about time he got himself a wider circle of friends, Alun thought.

"Something must have been blocking him," said Rhod, who seemed cross with himself.

"Well even the phone signal can be pretty bad in this part of Anglesey," Alun said. "Worth a try, I guess."

They both nodded at each other.

"Don used to talk a lot about malicious spirits in this hotel," said Rhod. "Apparently they can interfere with readings if they're trying to hide something."

Alun looked down at the burnt sausage still sitting on the plate and decided to take a bite. "I don't like the sound of a malicious ghost. The friendly ones are scary enough."

Rhod noticed the copy of the medium's old paperback lying by the bed. He seemed excited to have another fan. "Don was writing about it in his new book, actually."

"He was?" asked Alun with a mouthful of sausage meat.

"He used to tell me that certain locations almost have a spirit of their own. A setting can almost influence a person's behaviour — make them do things that they normally wouldn't. Objects and structures can possess as much energy as a human being."

"Like the Amityville house?"

Rhod was completely stumped. "The *what*?"

"Nothing. You should watch that film. I think you'd really like it."

Alun finished eating his snack and let the confused teenager continue.

"Don seemed to believe that there was a lot of darkness in this place. He hadn't seen anything like it since the time he visited an old prison somewhere in America. They say that enough pain and suffering in a place can compound into an evil energy that never goes away."

The last mouthful of Alun's sausage went down his throat like a piece of rock. He had endured more than enough "evil spirits" back at Pengower Lake, and he wasn't intending to repeat that experience anytime soon.

"Did he give any specifics?" he asked. "You know, actual events that might have happened."

A weariness grew on Rhod's face. "He had a whole list of historic events that spanned hundreds of years. There have been a lot of strange and suspicious deaths at Balamon."

"Tell me something I don't know!"

"But his opinion on a more recent one would have been quite controversial had he published the book." Alun hung on his every word. He had a feeling that what Rhod was about to reveal next might be quite significant. "He believed that the spirits of this hotel had driven people to commit murder on more than a few occasions, the most recent one being —"

A loud creak caused both of them to turn around. A familiar

voice spoke: "Not a good idea leaving your door unlocked — not at this hotel."

Standing in the open doorway was a confused Rhiannon. The sight of Alun sitting in a circle of candles with his young medium almost had her lost for words. "Oh, I'm sorry. Am I interrupting something?"

CHAPTER 24

Alun stared at the measly selection of breakfast cereals and couldn't help but feel disappointed. After his extravagant meal the night before, he had expected a banquet of fried food to choose from, including his usual favourites: black pudding, bacon, eggs and perhaps even a hash brown. Instead, he was presented with the most basic continental breakfast a person could cobble together (and there weren't even any croissants).

"Turns out the kitchen don't do breakfasts," Rhiannon muttered in his ear, as she leant forward and snatched up the last yoghurt. "Apparently Mark likes to sleep in."

"Lucky him," Alun muttered, and he decided to grab himself a bowl before an elderly couple jumped in front of him.

Carys Roden stood at the other end of the table with a proud look on her face. The breakfast buffet was all her responsibility, and this morning she had included the addition of her homemade bread (she was still working on the recipe).

Alun gave the assistant manager a reluctant nod as he went past. The dining hall was certainly more lively in the morning than it was the rest of the day. The Balamon's key demographic seemed to consist mainly of pensioners and young families who were all looking for a budget holiday. And at the Balamon, they were getting exactly what they paid for.

Rhiannon watched her fellow guest sitting himself down with a small bowl of shredded wheat. She had often wondered why people felt the need to eat so much breakfast when staying at a hotel. At home, a person would be quite satisfied with a slice of toast, and yet, on holiday, the opportunity of an all-you-can-eat buffet meant that they consumed until the point of nausea. Fortunately, at this hotel, people didn't need to worry about *that* problem.

"How's your stay going?" she asked.

Alun looked at her with a hungry frown, as though she already knew the answer. "I've had worse."

"I won't ask what you and your little friend were getting up to last night." She swallowed a mouthful of yoghurt. "Alright, actually I will — what in the devil's name were you two doing in there?"

"It was just an experiment," said Alun, poking at his dry piece of wheat.

Rhiannon was finding it very hard not to keep a straight face. "Well, whatever it was, I'm glad you didn't get *me* involved. Let me guess — did it involve moving furniture and falling ornaments?"

"Something like that."

"Say no more. We won't ever need to speak of it again."

"That would be good. Thanks."

"So *my* night, on the other hand..." She had an excited look on her face. It was the kind a small child had when they were struggling to keep a secret. "Turns out Don's new book would have been quite the page-turner."

Alun looked up from his bowl. She had his full attention now and was loving every minute of it.

"The missing manuscript?" he asked. "How would you know that?"

The reporter leaned across the table until her hair was almost in his milk. "Because I met someone who read it."

"Interesting. And there was me thinking you'd had an early night."

Rhiannon flung back her hair and pretended to blush. "That's just because of my youthful glow, darling."

Even in his grumpy mood, the accountant struggled not to find her amusing.

"So this book," she continued, pressing her finger against the table. "Our friend Don was about to drop some pretty big bombshells."

"I'm listening."

"The first one was his sexuality."

It had not been the reveal Alun had expected, but it surprised him nonetheless. "He was gay?"

"Turns out the man was bisexual. And he'd been hiding the fact his whole life." She seemed disappointed by her friend's lukewarm reaction. "Isn't that crazy?"

"Well, not really. We live in the twenty-first century. People come out all the time."

"Yes, but it would have been a big deal for people of his generation — especially, in middle America. He'd been suppressing a huge part of his identity, and he was finally going to go public in a new book."

Alun sighed. "I don't mean to sound harsh, but Don Fletcher's fanbase had dwindled quite a lot since the seventies. His book was hardly going to make the news."

"Well, I thought it was an interesting story," Rhiannon huffed. Despite the anticlimactic reveal, she was still sitting on another tantalising secret and was saving the best to last. "God, talk about a tough crowd. Alright, well how about this — turns out Mr Fletcher was going to spill the beans on something else. It sounds like there have been murders going on in this hotel long before even he arrived."

"Well it was a castle. They are known for their fair share of bloodshed." He almost yelped out, as she prodded her toe against his shin. It hadn't been hard, and he was glad not to have revealed his very low pain threshold.

"More recent than that!" Rhiannon cried, before realising how much she was raising her voice. She looked around the hall to make sure none of the other diners were listening. "Don was adamant that the death of Lady Margaret — Sir Dylan Pugh's first wife — was more than just a suicide. The popular belief is that she jumped out of a window. But Don had a string of theories on how she was pushed. And you'll never guess by who..."

"Her husband?"

Rhiannon's face dropped. His calm and collected expression made her want to grab her yoghurt and splatter it across the man's smug face.

"Uh, yes," she said. "How did you know that?"

"Rhod told me," said Alun. "We discussed it just after you barged in, actually. Don was studying the effect of malicious spirits. He believed Sir Dylan had been possessed at the time."

"Course he flaming did," said the deflated journalist. "And of course he blamed the ghosts. It's always their fault."

"You seem annoyed."

"I'm *not* annoyed!"

The hall went silent. Rhiannon realised the volume of her cry and mimed out an apology.

"Alright, Mr Know-it-all," she continued. "So what you're telling me is all this info is useless — is that it?"

"Well, not quite," said Alun, hoping to improve her mood. "It shows that there was at least *something* in that manuscript that a few people would want to keep private. A murder accusation would tarnish Sir Dylan's glowing reputation, and if there are more slanderous details in there, then it gives us a motive as to why someone would want to steal it."

His friend sighed. "I've also been trying to figure out this room key conundrum. I'm surprised you've not worked out a theory yet. You love that sort of dorky stuff."

"What's the conundrum?"

"Each room has two keys, right? Gwen would have had her own and Carys had the other."

"Did Carys definitely have the other one?"

They both looked towards the assistant manager, who was still standing guard at the breakfast buffet.

"Yes," said Rhiannon. "I checked with her on the way in. She used it to open the door the following morning. And we know what she found."

Alun nodded, and his mind began rooting through all the possibilities. "The only way that another killer would have made it inside is if they were let in. We've already established that. Also, if someone *was* let in, how would Johnny not have seen them? It doesn't make sense."

"Ah-ha!" Rhiannon slapped her hand against the table, causing her friend to jump, along with her bowl. "I've been thinking about this too!"

Alun watched in anticipation, as she began placing their eating utensils into a strange small-scale representation of Gwen's room. She picked up a sachet of ketchup and placed it into the square.

"This is Gwen, right?" she continued. Her single audience member very wisely decided to humour her. "Before she made her little booty call to Johnny —"

"Booty — *what*?"

His confusion resulted in an impatient sigh. "Gwen

messaged Johnny to come up to her room. Do you need me to explain the birds and the bees to you as well?"

"No, I've got that part down already, thank you very much." The accountant blushed and wished he'd never said anything.

"But before he got to her room, the real killer arrived at her door first."

"Okay..."

She picked up the salt shaker, which had now changed its purpose from seasoning to murder. "So she lets the killer inside —"

"Hold on — why would she do that?" Alun asked, clutching his forehead.

"Most murder victims know their killer. And most domestic killings are the result of the victim letting their killer inside. I don't know — perhaps she thought she could reason with them — or threaten them, even! Maybe she had the upper hand somehow. She was drunk as a skunk. People do stupid things." The salt shaker moved in between the square made from cutlery and was joined by an empty mini cereal box.

"What's that supposed to be?"

"Just be quiet!" Rhiannon snapped. "All will be revealed soon. Next, Gwen sends her killer packing. She asks him to leave and she rushes to the bathroom for... whatever she needs to do. But the killer doesn't actually leave the room!" She lifted up the salt shaker and placed it inside the cereal box. "She thinks the killer has left, but they're actually hiding underneath the bed."

Alun bit down on his lower lip and tried hard not to say anything.

"Then," the journalist continued, "Johnny comes along."

Now a pepper shaker made its way into the room. Rhiannon placed it, along with the sachet of ketchup, on top of the enormous bed. She decided not to try reenacting what would have happened next, especially not in a public place.

"Hours later," she said, "the killer climbed out from underneath the bed and..."

The salt shaker was lifted high into the air before it came crashing back down with a *splat*. Alun looked on in disbelief, as the force from Rhiannon's unexpected *slam* caused a spray of red sauce to fly out from the crushed sachet.

"Oh, sorry," Rhiannon said, realising what she had tried to mimic. "That was probably a bit much."

Alun looked around to check nobody had noticed. "Yes," he agreed. "I think it was a little inappropriate."

"But it's the only way it could have happened!" She saw him studying the desperation in her face and backed away.

"Why are you so desperate for it not to be him?"

His suspicious stare only made her even more frustrated. "Because Johnny didn't kill her! Why would he have done? Why would he take a hammer from reception, murder someone in cold blood and then wait to be caught? It just doesn't make sense!"

"Is everything alright for you?"

They both turned to see the assistant manager towering above their table with her signature grin.

"Oh, yes," said Rhiannon, licking up a blob of ketchup from her thumb. "It was lovely, thank you. Alun particularly enjoyed his, didn't you, Alun?"

The accountant looked down at his soggy cereal. "Oh, yes. It was lovely."

Rhiannon felt a vibration in her pocket. She pulled out her phone and saw an unknown caller coming up on her screen. "Please excuse me," she said. "I really need to take this."

CHAPTER 25

Rhiannon wished she had never answered. When the call had come through, her curiosity had got the better of her, once again. Now she was trapped on a call with a raving lunatic.

"It's not normal," said the high-pitched voice on the other end of the line. "I got you to eat everything when you were his age."

She had forgotten that her mother had started withholding calls. Morwenna Williams was catching on fast: if her name didn't appear, then her daughter was far more likely to answer.

"It's just potatoes, mam," Rhiannon groaned. "He's not going to starve. They're not even one of your five-a-day!"

"They're a vegetable as far as I'm concerned," said Morwenna. "Always have been, always will be."

Her daughter squeezed the phone, hoping it would disintegrate in her hand. A gentle morning mist hung in the air, and she could feel the condensation against the wall behind her. If it weren't for the pleasant view keeping her calm, she would have lost all patience.

"So how much longer is this jolly of yours going to last?" her mother asked.

"Not too much longer, I hope," Rhiannon answered. "And it's not a *jolly*. I have no desire to be here any longer than I have to, believe me." She leaned back against the hard stone and gazed up at the hotel's towering exterior. The building was almost grinning at her like a wicked captor. "I'm ready to go home. I really miss him."

She was struck by her own use of the word "home". It was the first time she had used it since moving back to Pengower. Did this mean that she had finally settled? Was she now a local? Heaven forbid, she thought.

"Well you *should* be missing him," the voice in her ear screeched. "The boy needs his mother. He also needs a father in his life, but don't get me started on that subject."

Rhiannon felt her blood pressure begin to rise. "I'm so glad I have you to point these things out to me. I'd be completely lost without your guidance."

The line went quiet. "Is that sarcasm I can hear? I hope not. I've only been looking after your son for days on end."

Here we go, Rhiannon thought. It was only a matter of time before she played the guilt card. Her mother loved having people in her pocket, and Rhiannon was as deep in that hole as you could possibly get.

"Oh," she said. "I think I'm losing you again. The reception really is terrible up here."

"Rhiannon, don't you dare!"

Her daughter lifted the phone high into the air, until Morwenna's voice was just a series of distant cries.

"Mam? Can you still hear me?"

She hung up the call and was surprised to find Alun standing there opposite her.

"Everything alright?" he asked.

"Terrific," Rhiannon replied. "So what's the plan?"

Alun looked out towards the gardens. "I thought we could take a look at the staff accommodation."

As they embarked on a pleasant morning stroll through the grounds, their attention was caught by a fluorescent figure in the middle of the front lawn.

"Wow," said Rhiannon. "*Someone's* a morning person."

The Balamon's resident health and fitness instructor was at the tail end of an hour-long yoga session. Dressed in bright purple spandex that could be seen from over a mile away, Billy finished his final pose and saw a familiar face through the narrow gap between his legs. With the world currently upside down in his downward dog position, he lowered himself back to the ground and gave a wave.

"Rhiannon!" he called out, before jogging over to her with the ease of a gazelle.

"Oh," she said, "hello."

His high energy at such an early hour made her cringe. Despite being a keen sporting enthusiast during her teens, she had since begun to loathe any form of cardiovascular activity and resented anyone who flaunted their own aerobic capacity.

"Owning the morning air, I see," said the over-enthusiastic Australian. "That's the way!"

"I wouldn't say we're quite *owning* it, but we thought a walk couldn't hurt."

Her heart sank, when she realised the man had decided to walk alongside them.

"Getting some steps in! Nice! I might join you."

"Great," Rhiannon muttered.

"So who's your friend?"

Alun endured a huge invasion of personal space.

"This is Alun. He's my... accountant."

She really needed to find a better description for her partner in crime, especially judging by the deflated look she was getting from him. But he *was* an accountant, and his name was indeed Alun. So that would have to do for now.

"Great to meet you, Al! My name's Billy. Hey, do you foam roll?"

"Uh, no. No, I don't. I'm not really a smoker."

"I thought not," said Billy, squeezing his shoulder. "You should come for a session down the spa. I reckon there's a lot of fascia we could be releasing."

"Alun would really love that, Billy." The evil look on Rhiannon's face made Alun shudder.

They headed further away from the hotel and came across a small tennis court with a net that looked like it had been ravaged by an angry wolf. The turf had worn to the point of being more suitable for a flower bed.

"Crying shame that," said Billy. "Old Robin puts his heart and soul into the gardens. But he couldn't give a toss about the sporting facilities. We need more team players around this place."

"You should mention it to Liz," said Rhiannon. "I'm sure there's plenty of funding."

The trainer kicked away a rotten tennis ball. "Nah. There's no way she's putting any money into this place. As soon as that mother of hers croaks it, she'll ditch this place quicker than her attention span."

"She might not need to wait long," said Alun. "Her inheritance from her other parent will be coming through soon."

It took Billy a moment, but once he'd thought about it, the trainer soon caught on.

"Ah! Yeah, that's right." He slapped the other man on the shoulder. "He's quick on the ball, your friend, Rhiannon! Of course — how could we forget about Daddy Don. Didn't see that one coming."

"You and Don were quite close, weren't you?" Rhiannon asked.

"As close as a masseuse and his client can be, I suppose," said Billy. "I'd say we got on quite well, sure."

"More than just friends?"

The trainer stopped walking. "Excuse me?"

Alun began to feel that oh-so-familiar feeling of discomfort.

"You wouldn't say that you and Don might have taken your relationship to the next level? I hear you have quite the reputation for playing the field around here."

Billy was gobsmacked. "Are you suggesting I seduced an old man?"

"Did you know he was gay?"

"Course I knew! I wasn't born yesterday. I know when a bloke is hiding something, and that one had it under lock and key. But just because there's two gay people in a room doesn't mean they want to rip each other's clothes off — anymore than two straight people. I never assumed you two were a couple."

Alun and Rhiannon both looked at each other. The awkwardness was clear.

"Oh, we're definitely not," said the journalist.

"No. Definitely not," said the accountant.

"Well, there you are!" cried the trainer. "Although... it's a crying shame. There's no denying the sexual tension going on between you two."

The other two looked at each other again, this time, for only a split second before distancing themselves.

Billy laughed. "I'm kidding!"

Alun let out a sigh of relief.

"I'm sorry," said Rhiannon. "I didn't mean to offend you."

Billy grabbed her by the shoulders and smiled. "Hey! I'm tougher than that, sweetheart. I've had a lot worse conversations than that in my time. Don't worry about it."

Just as they were about to continue their walk, a short man with long, white hair and a reflective coat came hurling through the bushes in a panicked frenzy. Rhiannon had seen this man on her arrival at the Balamon and recalled that he was a volunteer.

"Another one!" he cried. "There's been *another* one!!"

The onlookers watched, as he lifted up his garden fork and began stabbing the ground like an enraged madman.

"Don't mind him," Billy whispered to the concerned pair next to him. "There must be another mole on the loose. The guy's obsessed."

After piercing several holes in what was left of the tennis court, the sight of a fresh mound over in the distance sent him hurling towards it. Alun winced as the mole hill was soon decimated.

"This place never ceases to disturb me," Rhiannon said very matter-of-factly.

The trio continued on their merry way and eventually approached a long cottage nestled behind the walled gardens. The hotel's pointed rooftops could still be seen from the front gate and the surrounding grounds made it an idyllic home for anyone looking for some peace and quiet.

"Here we are," said Billy. "Our humble abode!"

Despite the tranquil setting, it was hard to ignore the blazing dance music coming from the second floor.

"Sounds like Mark's awake," he added. "A bit early for him. Fancy a cuppa?"

They entered through the front door and came across Gethin putting on his shoes. The concierge did not seem himself and displayed little of his usual confidence.

"Alright, Geth?" the trainer asked, almost enjoying the awkward moment a little too much.

"Uh, yes. I'm good." The man finished tying up his immaculate shoes and didn't even look the other staff member in the eye. He stood up and was even more surprised to find Alun and Rhiannon darkening his door. "What are you two doing here? These are private quarters."

Billy groaned and signalled for the other two to follow him into the kitchen. "Stop being an old stick in the mud. These are our guests." He raised his arms and put on his poshest accent. "I say, ladies and gentlemen, would you care to join me in our dining quarters?"

The concierge stormed off in a huff, which only amused the trainer even more.

Daylight poured through from the enormous double-hung window and landed across a floor of terracotta tiles. The kitchen had a rustic feel that reminded Alun of a Beatrix Potter illustration.

Sitting at the other end of the large oak table was Mared, sipping on a coffee and reading her magazine.

"Seems like *everyone's* an early bird this morning," said Billy, flicking on the kettle.

The young housekeeper didn't even bat an eyelid. "Only not everyone makes a song and dance about it," she muttered.

The trainer made a catlike screech and threw a teabag at her.

"And to what do we owe this pleasure?" said a husky, deep voice.

Mark entered the room in a pair of grubby pyjamas with a newspaper under his arm. The chef was bleary-eyed and had not long climbed out of bed.

Judging by his choice of music coming from upstairs, Rhiannon had decided that this was a man obsessed with reliving his youth. The fact he was living in a shared accommodation with people half his age didn't help.

"Someone was partying hard last night," said Billy.

The chef chuckled and plonked himself down at the table.

"I'll sleep when I'm dead." He eyed up the two visitors again. "Come to offer more compliments, have we?"

"Not really," said Rhiannon. She crossed her arms. "The kitchen can't seem to handle breakfast."

Mared let out a smirk, as the man taking over her table grunted. "What were you celebrating?" she asked him.

Mark lent forward, or, at least, as much as his large midriff would allow. "Life, my dear."

"Well, some do seem to have it better than others."

Another grunt followed.

The journalist observed the social dynamics of these three unlikely housemates with great intrigue. It appeared the chef was as unpopular among his fellow staff as she'd predicted, which was going to make her next question a lot easier: "Tell me, chef, why is it you were staying in the hotel room opposite Gwen's the night before last? When you only live a short walk away?"

Mark twisted himself around to look at her.

Alun looked up towards the ceiling and clenched all of his own muscles (not that there was much to clench). The sudden tension in the room was killing him.

"Like you just pointed out — because it saved me a walk," said the chef, firmly. "And if you're going to start all this private eye nonsense on me again, you can sling your hook."

"Is it true that you and Don Fletcher fell out?" she asked again.

Alun was running out of muscles to tighten.

"Anyone who criticises my food needs their taste buds testing!" boomed the hungover chef.

"I heard that he sent the food back on many occasions."

Mark glared at her and decided not to be provoked. It was exactly what she wanted. Instead, he laughed in her face and turned his attention to the morning newspaper. When he opened the first page, his eyes widened.

"Well, I never!" he said.

The entire room gathered around the table to see what he had seen. Spread out across two pages was a story about a local serial killer.

"They charged him..." Alun said, echoing the exact thoughts on everyone's mind.

The headline read: *Merchant of death*. Underneath was the sentence: *Local funeral director charged for the murder of four people.*

"*Four*?!" Mared cried.

Rhiannon remained silent and stared in disbelief at the image of Johnny Roberts.

CHAPTER 26

"Four murders..." Alun shook his head, as he strolled back towards the hotel. "I never could have imagined that."

Rhiannon had been silent since they had left the staff cottage. She was lost in a trail of thought that felt like a bottomless, dark hole. The names of all those local victims flashed through her mind: *Huw Earnshaw, Sara Jarrett, Nerys Wilkinson, Gwen Tudor...* They had been typed out in a cold, familiar font that she knew so well, having used it countless times herself.

"I feel so stupid," she eventually said.

Alun turned to her, relieved to hear another person speak. "I wouldn't be too hard on yourself. He had everyone fooled by the sounds of it. They said he'd started committing those crimes way before we got here. He should have been caught sooner. It wasn't like you tried to help the man."

She turned to look at him. He saw her guilty expression. It was the one he knew very well by this point, and they had reached a stage where no words needed to be said.

"Oh," he said. "Oh, please tell me you didn't..."

Rhiannon dropped to her knees and sat herself down by the

side of the path. "The man called me on my mobile! He swore he was innocent. And I believed him!"

"When was this?" Alun asked, deciding to join her on the ground (albeit rather reluctantly, judging by the dampness of the grass and the brightness of his carefully ironed trousers).

"Last night... He seemed adamant he hadn't killed her."

"Well, maybe he didn't."

She lifted up her head, which, until now, had been buried in her hands.

"This doesn't change the fact that Gwen's murder was any less strange," he continued. "According to the press, Johnny had killed three other people and got away with it. Why make such a stupid mistake on the fourth?"

Rhiannon could have hugged him right there and then. Even if he didn't mean what he was saying, it gave her at least *some* comfort. He may have been the strangest man she knew, but he knew exactly how to make her feel better.

"Maybe I've been focused on the wrong murder," she said, looking over towards the hotel. It loomed up in the distance, like the fortress that it once was, all those centuries ago. "I don't know whether Don Fletcher's theories on evil spirits are true, but there's definitely been some dark deeds going on in there."

Alun climbed to his feet. "Then maybe we should talk to the person who knew Don the most. He did bring us here in the first place. I guess it's time we help him get to the bottom of his friend's death."

The journalist nodded. She knew exactly who he was referring to.

~

RHOD SHUFFLED NERVOUSLY in his seat. *The Hafan Cafe* in Tremor was deathly quiet. The sudden downpour of rain outside hadn't helped matters, as it had sent any visiting tourist back to their tents and holiday homes.

The teenager was joined by Alun and Rhiannon, who sat opposite him with grave faces.

"I assume you've heard about the news," said the journalist.

Rhod nodded.

"I'm so sorry, Rhod," Alun added. "I can't imagine the shock of it all."

"It was no shock," said Rhod. "It was me who provided the evidence."

The other two people on his table looked at each other. "You did — *what*?"

The young man nursed his cup of coffee and stared into the melting chocolate powder. "I've had my suspicions for a while," he said. "The business has really been struggling for the last few years. People around here seemed to be living longer, and with a new funeral directors down the road, we didn't stand a chance." He took his teaspoon and prepared himself a mouthful of white froth. "My father had a good relationship with people in this village. He knew everyone. And when someone needed a funeral, we'd be the first place they came. My brother, on the other hand, wasn't nearly as popular. You could say he was pretty antisocial, actually, and got into all sorts of trouble growing up."

Rhiannon shook her head in disbelief. "Wait, are you telling me Johnny murdered people to help his family business? A business that happened to profit from people's deaths?"

"You couldn't write it," Alun said, equally shocked. "I suppose it does make sense in a strange way." He saw the look of judgement coming from Rhiannon. "In a dark and twisted way, I mean."

"It's sick is what it is," she said and then remembered who was with them. "No offence to you, obviously."

Rhod nodded at her. "It's alright. None taken." He let out a nervous cough and took another sip of coffee.

"So when did you begin to clock that these deaths were suspicious?" Alun asked. "Clearly the police hadn't noticed."

"That's where my brother was clever," said Rhod. "Or maybe not so clever in the end, but, anyway — he targeted people who were vulnerable, people he came across through his side business."

"That sounds like a very foolish move to me," said Rhiannon. "The hardest serial killers to catch are the ones who pick their victims at random — with no pattern — which happens to be rarely the case."

Alun couldn't help but wonder how his friend knew so much about serial killers but decided that now wasn't the time to ask.

Rhod shrugged. "This pattern was how I first caught on to what he was doing. The names of each new funeral client was always linked to a job we'd done at some point or to the places he worked, like our father's care home. That was where the second to last victim lived."

"*Second*-to-last?" asked Rhiannon. "Wait, who was the last?"

"Gwen Tudor."

"Oh. Yes, that's right."

"Before Johnny's arrest, I'd found a little scrapbook he'd made. It had everything: the names of the victims, business receipts – even condolence letters to the family members. I was going to confront him about it when we got back from the party."

"It was brave of you to turn him in like that," Alun told him.

The teenager stared at the raindrops crawling down the window. On the other side of the glass was the harbour, which, on this rainy summer's day, had lost all hint of colour.

"It wasn't bravery," he said. "I was afraid. I'd held the burden of his secret for long enough. I needed to set myself free. It's not easy knowing your brother's a psychopath and being too scared to say anything."

"Well, you did the right thing," said Rhiannon, grabbing hold of his hand.

Rhod appreciated the gesture. "I wanted to apologise to you both, actually. I feel like I brought you all this way for nothing."

The other two smiled at each other.

"Oh, I wouldn't say that," said Alun. "My friend here's got herself a story to go back with. And we're not finished here yet..."

His last sentence gave the teenager a glimmer of hope.

"Really?" he asked.

Rhiannon nodded. "There's still another killer on the loose. And right now, only the walls of the *Balamon Hotel* knows who that is. But I think we're going to need your help."

The rain had finally eased off by the time the caffeinated trio emerged onto the shores of Tremor. As they left the cosy warmth of the *Hafan Cafe*, a familiar figure was making his way towards them along the harbour.

"Fancy seeing you here," said the gardener, directing his words towards Alun, who greeted him with a nod.

"Robin," he said, after taking a moment to remember the face. The man he had first seen in the Balamon gardens seemed strangely out of place out there in the village. This white-haired man in grubby clothes was no longer camouflaged by his natural habitat.

"Just thought I'd pay poor Rowena a visit," said Robin. "Offer her my condolences in the flesh." He waved the newspaper in his hand. "Terrible business all this, eh? If one tragedy wasn't enough."

"Rowena Tudor?" Rhiannon asked. "She lives near here?"

"Of course. She's just over there —"

The gardener pointed towards a pink terraced house further down the road. Although the view would have been nice, the building itself had seen much better days, and its paint was riddled with brown patches.

Rhiannon was surprised by such a humble home and already admired the woman. "Looks like her inheritance didn't go very far."

"Rowena has no interest in money, I can assure you," said Robin. "She's always wanted to make her own way in life. And good on her! I admire that."

The journalist turned to her two companions. "Maybe we should pay our own respects."

"That's very kind," said the gardener. "I'm sure she'll appreciate that."

The man tipped his flat cap and continued on his way.

Alun had a bad feeling about their next move.

"Are you sure this is a good idea?" he asked, as they approached the front door. "The woman's only just lost her daughter to a deranged serial killer. She's probably not in the mood for a chat with us."

"Mmmm," said Rhiannon, taking his point on board. "You might be right about the serial killer part." She turned to face Rhod. "You! Wait over there." The confused teenager followed her pointed finger, which seemed to be directed at the sea. "We can't have her daughter's killer's brother hanging around. It might cause some offence."

Rhod respected her wishes, and, like an unwanted puppy, walked away towards the seafront.

"That wasn't exactly what I meant," Alun muttered to her through gritted teeth.

He reluctantly joined her on the doorstep.

"If anyone knows the darkest secrets of that hotel it's the rightful heir," said a determined Rhiannon. She gave a firm *knock* and hoped for the best.

When the door finally opened, they were greeted with a person they had not expected.

"Oh..."

The young woman standing in the doorway stared back at the baffled journalist with sheer amusement. "Can I help you?" she asked.

"I'm sorry," Rhiannon replied, who wasn't normally so lost for words. "We were expecting Rowena Tudor."

"And?"

"Well, uh... Is this not her house?"

"Yeah, this is her house."

Standing at the door was Mared, the Balamon's housekeeper and occasional barmaid. She folded her arms and delivered a statement that was even more surprising than her appearance: "I'm her daughter."

CHAPTER 27

"Don't you walk away from me, girl!"

Mared was joined at the door by a furious woman in a pair of dungarees covered in paint.

"Looks like you've got company," said Mared, who pointed at the two visitors standing in her front garden. Alun and Rhiannon cleared a space to allow the determined daughter to storm off towards the gate.

With her orders disobeyed, the older woman turned her attention to the gawking strangers.

"Rowena Tudor, I presume?" Rhiannon asked.

"Who's asking?" Rowena snapped. "In fact, don't bother answering. I just want to be left alone."

"We know this is probably a painful time for you, Mrs Tudor, but —"

"Don't give me that spiel! I don't even know the pair of you! I've had enough of you bottom-feeders for one day. Nobody ever came knocking at my door before..." She seemed on the verge of tears but held on tight. "Now every man and his dog wants to speak to me!"

Alun decided it was time to intervene. He pulled out a handkerchief and offered it to her. "We didn't mean to upset you. We're quite happy to leave if you would prefer. My name's Alun and this is Rhiannon. We got to know Gwen a little during our stay at the Balamon. My friend here tried to help her. She even rescued her from a sauna accident."

Rowena Tudor declined the handkerchief (which Rhiannon was still in awe that he owned such a thing), and she headed inside the house with the door left ajar.

Alun hesitated as to whether to follow, until his journalist friend assured him that this was a sign that they definitely should.

The walk to the living room was a short one. The house was slightly larger than expected on the inside, but its ground floor consisted of little more than two rooms and a narrow hallway beside the staircase.

Rowena positioned herself back in front of a tall easel in the middle of the small space. Paint was splattered across the floor with not a dust sheet in sight. As far as the obsessive-compulsive accountant was concerned, it was far worse than any crime scene.

"We're sorry to interrupt your... painting," Rhiannon said, choosing her last word very carefully. The canvas had been massacred with every colour at the woman's disposal, and it was unlike any painting she had ever seen (not that she was an expert).

"It's strange what grief does to you," said Rowena, picking up her brush and flinging another splash of colour. "It changes every hour. But right this second I have a strange urge to paint."

"They say art is just an expression of emotion," said Alun. "It covers a whole spectrum of different feelings."

Rhiannon turned to him with a cynical frown and wondered who this man was that had just taken over her friend's body.

"I'm no artist, or anything," he added. "But I read it in a magazine at the dentist once."

Thank goodness for that, Rhiannon thought to herself. For a minute, she had thought she'd lost him.

"We're all artists," said Rowena, who was taking a liking to this smartly dressed man. "I just needed to take my mind off things for an hour."

Alun watched another flicker of paint spray across the floorboards near his polished shoes and took a step back.

"So, you rescued my daughter from a sauna?" Rowena asked, turning to face Rhiannon.

"Uh, yes. Sort of. We found her locked inside one over at the hotel spa. That's when she told us about the death threats."

"She never said anything to me. But I'm only her mother. As you probably saw at the door, my daughter's can be quite a handful."

Rhiannon moved herself over to the fireplace so she didn't have to look at the woman's handy work. It was already starting to make her feel queasy. "Actually, I had no idea Mared was Gwen's sister until just now."

"You couldn't get two sisters more different than those two. It was obvious from when they were children: one liked barbies and dressing up, whilst the other took after her mother."

Alun tried to work out which one was supposed to be which, but the answer soon became clear.

"Mared certainly inherited the artistic gene," Rowena continued. "Not that we've ever got along that well. I thought this whole tragedy would at least bring us closer together. But nothing quite turns out how you think it's going to."

"I'm sure you're both still hurting," said Alun.

"She has her own, unique way of conveying her emotions, that one — Mared, I mean. But, then again, so do I."

Her visitors flinched at the next paint explosion.

Rhiannon leaned herself against the fireplace and came across a row of framed photographs. She saw two girls playing together near a pond.

"I'm surprised they both ended up working at the hotel," she said. "That must have been strange for you."

Rowena saw her looking at the photograph. "If there's one thing they *have* always had in common, it's rebelling against their mother."

"I'm sure I've seen this exact pond over in the hotel gardens."

"They used to spend most of their summers running around that place. My father was still alive then, and they loved going there. I suppose it's a nice place when you don't have a load of emotional baggage tied to it."

"Your father being Sir Dylan Pugh?"

"Oh, don't forget the *Sir*," Rowena said with a scoff. "He was a loving grandfather but a strict father. Then he let that witch in through the front door and he became even worse."

Her listeners tried not to dwell too much on the word "witch". They'd had enough of those.

"Yes, we've had the pleasure of meeting Lady Angela," said Rhiannon. "Such a charmer."

"She put a charm on him, that's for sure. Now she's bleeding him dry to this very day."

"You must have only been a child when she arrived on the scene?"

The woman lowered her brush and appeared to be reliving a painful memory.

"Which made me all the more helpless," she said. "They talk about wicked stepmothers in the fairytales, well, Hansel and Gretel didn't know they were born."

Alun walked over to the photographs and picked up the oldest one of them all. "Is this your mother, Margaret?"

Rowena gave him a suspicious frown. "You two seem to know a lot about my family. Who did you both say you were again?"

The accountant almost dropped the photograph and hugged it tight. "Uh, well we —"

"Do you remember much about Don Fletcher?" Rhiannon asked, before her friend could say anything that would make their situation worse.

"I think you better leave," Rowena insisted. "Unless you're another long lost relative, I've got nothing more to say."

"But you *do* remember him? You know, the psychic? The ghost lover?"

"He's dead. Just like everyone else from that time in my life — whether they're still breathing or not. They're all dead to me."

Just as Rhiannon was about to press the woman further, Alun desperately tried to get her attention.

"I think we need to make a move," he said, pointing towards the window.

She ignored his warning and approached the easel with remarkable bravery.

"Don had made some quite serious allegations about your family, and I wondered if you would mind confirming a couple for us —"

"Rhiannon!" Alun said firmly, his hands now grabbing her shoulders as he blocked her path. "We need to go! Now!"

She was just about to make him pay dearly for getting in her way, when she saw what he had been looking at. Through the bay window overlooking the seafront, they could see a helpless Rhod being manhandled by a furious Mared.

"Oh," said Rhiannon and decided to grant her friend's wishes. "Thank you for your time, Mrs Tudor!"

Rowena's front door went bursting open, and the two visitors came charging out as fast as they could run.

Unfortunately for Rhod, they were too late to prevent his

bloodied nose, and his attacker was already making her way back towards the harbour.

"What happened?" Alun asked, holding the teenager's head up to stop the bleeding.

"I should probably get used to it," Rhod whimpered. "It's not going to be easy having your brother known as a convicted serial killer." He straightened his coat, which the young woman had managed to tear only moments before. "She started asking me if I knew what Johnny had been doing all this time. Said I could have prevented her sister's murder. I was too scared to answer, so she punched me."

"Your psychic powers didn't see that one coming then?" Rhiannon asked, much to the disapproval of Alun.

"We shouldn't have left you alone out here," he said.

Rhiannon pointed in the direction of Rowena's house. "I don't think it would have been much safer in there."

They all started walking back towards the main harbour. Mared had long gone, and the sun began poking its way out from behind one of the dark clouds.

"Where to now?" Rhiannon asked.

Alun took one last look at the pink house before they reached her car. "Where this whole fiasco started," he said. "The scene of the crime."

∼

DON FLETCHER'S hotel room was exactly how they had left it. Carys, the assistant manager, led the trio inside. Unlike the concierge, she had been quite happy to allow access without the need for a cash payment and was quite willing to assist in their investigation, especially if there was a chance that her former guest had met his maker through the means of foul play. There was nothing to hide, as she so finely put it.

Ironically, hiding something would have been quite easy in those mountains of clutter that the old medium had left behind.

"And you placed the tray down *here*," Alun said to her, placing his imaginary hot chocolate delivery on the desk.

"Yes," said Carys, full of her usual nervous energy. "Mr Fletcher had his hot chocolate brought up for exactly eight o'clock every night."

Alun nodded, whilst Rhiannon and Rhod observed their conversation with great intrigue.

"And how long before you noticed the suicide letter?" he asked.

Carys scratched through her fluffy perm. "Well, as soon as he didn't answer my calls. He usually takes his bubble bath at this time and he likes it brought to him, so I checked if he was ready for me.

"He had you bring it to him whilst he was in the bath?" Rhiannon interjected.

"Oh, don't worry, dear," Carys said with a giggle. "It was all quite innocent. Don used a lot of bubble bath. You would never see a thing."

The journalist didn't seem so sure, but if someone else wanted to take the risk then it was up to them.

"So you didn't hear a reply?" Alun asked, trying to keep things on track.

"Not a peep from him," Carys replied. "I called a few times and that's when I saw the letter. I'd always told him to keep the bathroom door unlocked. You can't be too careful with a person of his age. Even my age, for that matter. Bathrooms are a dangerous place."

"Clearly," said Rhiannon.

"I went to the door and that's when I saw his feet," the assistant manager continued. "I could see them floating from the doorway."

They all gathered inside the bathroom. It was hard to imagine such a scene at this point. The bath was now empty and everything seemed calm.

"And it was at that point you screamed?"

Carys looked at the accountant, almost surprised that he knew. "Why, yes. I did."

Alun paced up and down, his hands clasped behind his back like a consulting doctor. "How fresh were the bubbles? Had they melted?"

"No, they were as fresh as anything, as if they'd just been created."

"So we can take it that he must have died right before you got there."

"Not unless someone added the bubbles after he died," Rhiannon pointed out.

"Why would they do that?" Alun asked, secretly impressed.

Rhiannon shrugged. "Just saying. You can't *assume* anything, Alun."

The accountant rolled his eyes at the sound of his own advice being repeated back to him. He stared down into the empty bath and, as his mind whirled, like water into an empty plug hole, something came to him.

CHAPTER 28

"The plug hole..." Alun stared down into the circular grate. "What is it that's bothering me about the plug hole?"

The other three stared at him. They had less of an idea than he did.

"What are you on about?" Rhiannon asked.

Alun shook his head. "I don't know. Something that struck me last time. Maybe it'll come to me."

"Well, whilst your little subconscious is working on that, how about we carry on with the task in hand?"

They were all lined up at the edge of the bathtub. Alun climbed inside and lay down in the same position Don would have been. He remained silent and listened to the dripping of a loose tap.

"Were there any particular sounds you could hear?" he asked the assistant manager.

Carys tried to ignore the fact that he was asking her whilst lying in an empty bath. "Well, it was very stormy that night."

Her words seemed to reinvigorate the relaxed man.

"A storm?" he asked, sitting up like a disturbed vampire.

"Why, yes. It was a terrible one. There were power cuts everywhere."

"But not here? Not at the hotel?"

"No," Carys assured him. "We had a flicker of lights but nothing more than that. Is it relevant?"

"It might well be," said Alun, his face distant.

Rhiannon was losing patience — fast. "Will you stop acting so strange and come on out with it? What are you thinking?"

The accountant climbed out of the bath (as smoothly as a person could climb out of an empty bath) and headed back into the bedroom.

"I need that staff rota," he called out.

Carys, Rhod and Rhiannon all looked at each other before joining him in the next room.

The man was searching under the bed when they walked in.

"What are you looking for?" Rhiannon asked.

"Nothing by the looks of it," he said.

Carys handed him a sheet of paper with a list of names. "This is everyone who was on duty."

Alun scanned the names: *Gethin Murray, Mark Stone, Rhys Gruffudd, Mared Tudor, Carys Roden, Sion Ifan, Manon Celyn, Sioned Evans.*

He recognised most of them, but there were three that eluded him.

"We were pretty short staffed that night," said Carys.

"Who are these last three names?" Alun asked.

"Sion's our pot washer and kitchen hand. Manon is front of house in the restaurant, but she was floating that night."

"Floating?"

"Many of our staff are floaters. It means they can do multiple duties in a shift."

Someone was definitely floating that night, Rhiannon thought.

"And Sioned?"

"She's front of house. I had her jump on reception when I went to bring up Don's hot chocolate."

Alun nodded, digesting the sheet of information like a human fax machine. "Mared was first on the scene when you called for help? Is that right?"

Carys nodded. "I'd say it was more of a scream than a call."

"And where was Liz?" Rhiannon asked.

"She had the night off to take her mother to a concert in Llangefni."

"What time did that finish?"

"I can't be sure."

Alun and Rhiannon shared the same look. They would certainly be checking that.

"I think we've taken enough of your time, Mrs Roden," Alun said to her.

The assistant manager handed him the room key. "Drop it off at reception when you're finished," she said. "I'm sure you can be trusted to leave this room how you found it?"

She gave them all a friendly wink, and they returned it with some appreciative smiles. Once she'd closed the door behind her, the others were left to ponder in silence.

"Well, I'm stumped," Rhiannon eventually said. "I don't know about you two, but I'm no closer to solving this one."

"What if..."

The other two turned to look at the teenager, who seemed to be on the verge of a theory.

"Never mind," he said.

Rhod looked up to see that he still had their full attention.

"Go on," said Alun.

The young man was sitting on the bed, his large boots tapping away against the carpet. "What if Don was right?"

His audience was still waiting for more details.

"What if," he continued, "there really *was* a dark spirit trying to kill him?"

Rhiannon groaned with disappointment. "Great, so it all comes back to the ghosts. This lad's obsessed."

Rhod wanted nothing more than to shrivel back into his shell, but he was also dying to make his point. "That doesn't mean it can't be a human killer. A dark spirit can take over their chosen subject, but they have to be susceptible enough."

"What are you saying?" Rhiannon asked. "We find the staff member most likely to be influenced by a demon spirit?"

"Well, sort of, yes."

The journalist collapsed against the bed with another groan. "Nice. Solid plan, Batman. We'll just go around sprinkling holy water and see if someone burns, shall we?"

"That's a good point," said Alun. Now it was his turn to have all eyes on him. "Water... Gwen said the person she saw leaving this room was covered in foam and water."

"So?" asked Rhiannon.

"If any of the staff members on duty had committed the crime, then it would have been obvious they were soaked. Meaning they would either have to change in a hurry, or —"

"It was someone not on duty," said Rhiannon.

"Exactly."

Rhod raised his hand. "But wasn't there a storm outside? It would have been quite easy to get drenched."

Rhiannon crawled over the duvet and pointed at him. "Why do you have to go and spoil everything?"

Alun smiled at him. "Don't worry, she's only joking with you."

The journalist gave him a dirty look of her own. "You reckon?" She leaped off the bed and stretched out her arms. "So I guess that means we're back to the evil spirits theory. You think a ghost typed up the man's suicide letter, too?"

They all looked over at the typewriter.

"Somebody did," said Alun, approaching the old-fashioned word processor and admiring its keys. His attention soon turned to the sliding sash window nearby, which had a similar view to his own room. He inspected the frame and saw that it could indeed open, if required.

Rhiannon and Rhod watched him struggle with the worn pulley system, until he heard the sweet grazing sound of wood on wood. The lower panes of glass slid upwards, and a gush of fresh air filled the room.

Alun stuck his head out to find that the ground below was much further than he had anticipated, and he felt a dizziness that hadn't presented itself since the fairground had come to Pengower. Even a ferris wheel had tested his nerves, and the prospect of falling two storeys was not an inviting one.

"Found anything yet?" Rhiannon's call was faint, but still loud enough that he bumped his head. "I don't think you'll find any murderers out *there!*"

He ignored her cries and saw a man in a hi-vis jacket go running across the gravel with his arms flailing.

"Help! Help!" cried the volunteer. "Someone help!"

Alun pulled himself back inside and went charging towards the door in a fit of panic.

A perplexed Rhiannon and Rhod looked at each other. "Where's he going?" she asked.

Before they both knew it, their friend was already descending the last staircase as fast as his puny limbs would allow. When he reached the front driveway, the volunteer gardener had amassed a small and curious crowd.

"It's enormous!" he cried. "This must be the biggest mole hill I've ever seen!"

Despite being concerned for the man's mental wellbeing, Alun and the small crew of staff members felt that they had little choice but to follow this distressed individual across the lawn.

Once they had reached the other side, even the sceptical followers had spotted what could not be refuted as a giant mound of earth.

"Someone's been digging where they shouldn't," said Robin, who joined them all with his wheelbarrow full of tools.

"I told you!" cried the volunteer. "This is the biggest mole ever!"

Alun ignored the warnings of a giant earth critter and walked over to inspect the mound. It was certainly fresh, and had all the hallmarks of something buried underneath.

"We should probably find out what's down there," he said to the small mob.

Still angry at the destruction of his perfect lawn, Robin threw him a shovel. The accountant looked at the tool as though he had never even seen one before and was getting very concerned about his shoes.

Rhiannon and Rhod wandered over to the small gathering and were surprised to find their friend with rolled-up sleeves and a concerned expression. They watched in admiration as he made his best attempt to hack away at the pile of earth like a bird pecking at a frozen apple crumble.

Robin could only watch for so long until he snatched the shovel back off him and showed everyone how it was done. The determined gardener grunted and huffed his way through the dirt, his face dripping with sweat, almost as much as Alun's was after only a few shovels.

The hole became deeper and deeper, and as the anticipation steadily grew, a different sound could soon be heard.

Robin tapped the edge of his shovel against something a lot more solid than loose soil. He reached out his rough hand and pulled up a package wrapped in brown paper.

A feeling of relief had struck many members of the curious bystanders. The sight of a solid object was far better than that of any human remains, something they had grown to expect after the last few days.

"This belong to anyone?" the gardener asked.

After enough shaking heads, he began tearing the outer layer of paper and revealed its mysterious contents. A moment later, Robin was holding up a bundle of tattered pages. The pile was as thick as a decent-sized novel, and, still within reaching distance, Alun read through the words on the first page.

"It's Don Fletcher's manuscript," he said, not quite believing his own words.

"Well that was an anticlimax," Robin muttered, and he handed him the pile as though its value had just plummeted.

Even the crowd of onlookers were very disappointed, all with the exception of Rhiannon and Rhod.

"Right, show's over, folks."

With the gardener's announcement still hanging in the air, Alun and his two friends were left alone with the unexpected find.

"Is the whole thing intact?" Rhiannon asked, huddled around the manuscript with excited eyes.

"Seems to be," said Alun.

The journalist could tell that something was bothering him. "What is it?"

"I don't know," he said, inspecting the first few pages. "Something doesn't feel right about this."

"What? The fact you've got dirt under your fingernails?"

Alun ignored her cheeky smile and continued to flick through the pages.

"Who wants to read it first?" asked Rhod, beaming with excitement, as if they'd found the holy grail.

"Calm down, fanboy," Rhiannon said to him. "We could be

holding a piece of evidence here. There'll be plenty of time to dribble over your hero's last book when we've worked out who put it here."

The teenager gave her a reluctant nod. "Who do we think *did* put this here?"

"The same person who took it after they murdered Don Fletcher," said Alun. "And there's only one way to confirm that." The other two gawked at him, dying to hear the answer. "I'm quite sure that the answers we're looking for are all inside this book."

He lifted up the manuscript, and they gathered around, like weary travellers studying an old map.

"I think we've got some reading to do."

CHAPTER 29

Alun lowered the final page of Don Fletcher's manuscript and placed it on the floor. Rhiannon and Rhod were sat either side of him with their backs against the bed, their faces tired and weary.

They had all spent the entire night in Alun's room, pouring over the enormous pile of pages in an effort to read the entire thing.

"Satisfied?" Rhiannon asked.

Her accountant friend straightened his sore back and nodded.

"So what now?" Rhod asked, wiping down his glasses.

"We call a staff meeting," said Alun. "Right after we've notified the police."

∽

THE DINING HALL had never been so over-staffed. All members of the *Balamon Hotel* rota were gathered together for the first time since the eventful birthday party, and something was telling them that they were in for another show.

Joining them this time, however, was a certain detective chief inspector and his local bobby, Officer Gwent, who were also curious about why they had been invited to the impromptu meeting.

Alun was positioned front and centre, and he would have been lying if he had said that nerves were not starting to creep in. Public speaking was not something he particularly enjoyed, and if it weren't for his two friends standing on either side of him, he would have abandoned the whole idea in an instant.

Rhiannon and Rhod both glanced at each other with the same feeling. They were a lot less confident than Alun about everything that was about to be said and hoped that the accountant had all of his facts straight.

All three of them looked around the room at the familiar faces: Gethin, the concierge; Liz Pugh, the manager; Carys, her assistant manager; Robin, the gardener; Billy, the trainer; Mark, the chef; Rhys, his assistant; Guto, the volunteer gardener; Mared, the housekeeper. Even Angela Pugh had come downstairs for this one. Over the course of the last week, they had got to know most of the hotel's workforce. It was quite the gathering, but it was the arrival of the final guest that really turned everybody's heads.

"What is *she* doing here?" asked Liz, over the chorus of whispers.

"I invited her," said Rhiannon, who was within earshot of the furious manager. "I thought she might be interested in hearing this, considering it's related to her daughter.

The room was getting impatient, and Alun decided it was time to clear his throat.

"Is everyone here?" he asked, turning to the wall of curious eyes.

"What's this all about?" croaked a restless Angela Pugh.

"All will soon be revealed," Rhiannon answered, enjoying the opportunity to silence her. "Please be patient."

Alun stepped forward, his hands clasped together in an effort to stop them shaking.

"Thank you all for coming at such short notice," he said with a cough. "I'm sure everyone is still in shock after the recent tragedy in room twenty-eight. But there was another terrible event that happened not too long before that." He could see the detective in the corner of his eye, who appeared to be listening intently. "Don Fletcher was a man most of you knew quite well — *very* well, some of you." This time it was Liz and Angela in his peripheral vision. "What all of you *didn't* know — or, at least, all but one person in this room — is that he was murdered in cold blood."

A wave of gasps and muttering forced him to pause for a moment, and he waited for the shock to die down.

"There's no turning back now," Rhiannon whispered to him.

Alun inhaled a deep breath of courage and prepared to continue. "You all might have been under the impression that Don had taken his own life on that stormy night, here at the hotel. But it wasn't the extra strong opioid that was responsible for his drowning; it was the actions of his determined killer, holding him down in the water. Being a frail man, who abused his body with alcohol and morphine on a regular basis, his murder could have well have been mistaken for a tragic suicide. But the *real* culprit behind Don's death had made some sloppy errors in judgement — almost as sloppy as the murder itself."

He rotated on the spot like a magician about to reveal a trick. The numerous faces hung on his every word, many of them desperate for him to unmask this supposed new killer walking among them.

"Whether it's the act of an evil spirit, a genetic instinct or an uncontrollable emotional outburst, we all have the capability to take a life. But it's not everyone who decides to act. If there's one thing I've learned during my visit to the *Balamon Hotel*, it's that murder may well be hereditary." He now turned to direct his next sentence to the murderer in question. "Isn't that right, Rhod?"

The entire room skipped a breath. They all turned their attention to the teenager standing beside their speaker, and nobody was more surprised than the young man himself.

"It's true, isn't it?" Alun continued. "It was *you* who Gwen saw leaving Don's room that night, covered in bath foam. It was you who buried this manuscript for us to find. It was you who drowned an elderly man who was too drug-induced to fight back."

"Stop it!!" Rhod cried, covering up his ears.

"Mr Hughes," said a deep voice. Alun turned to see DCI Neale stepping forward. "I do hope you're going to elaborate. The young man is quite distressed, and this is quite a serious accusation you're making."

Alun signalled for Rhiannon to pass him the manuscript.

"I should probably point out the fact that my friend was invited here under the impression she was meeting Don Fletcher himself. It turns out that the person who really brought her here — the person standing beside me right now — had not only forged his e-mails, but had also forged an entire autobiography. And therefore a man's legacy."

He lifted up the manuscript and Rhiannon held up a page she had already pulled out.

"This teenager clearly has some talents when it comes to summoning the dead," she announced. "But his spelling and grammar have a lot to be desired." She pulled out an e-mail printout from her pocket. The document was littered with red marks. "The spelling mistake in this manuscript is the same as the one found in a certain e-mail correspondence."

"*Receave*," Rhiannon confirmed. "*Receive* is quite a commonly misspelt word. But it's quite rare to find it missing an 'i'."

"The moment this manuscript was dug up yesterday afternoon, something troubled me," said Alun. "It was almost as if someone had wanted us to find it. And why would someone hide a person's personal memoirs, only to then have them found again? There could only be one solution."

"It was a different manuscript," Rhiannon added. "We'd originally thought that someone had hidden Don's unpublished work to preserve another person's reputation. But it wasn't anyone *else's* public image that they were concerned about; it was Don Fletcher's." She walked over to Mared and pointed. "As one of the few people to have had the pleasure of reading Don's original draft, Mared very kindly dished out what she believed were the juicy elements: Don's true sexuality, his suspicion of murder and corruption within the Pugh family, his affair with Lady Angela. But another focus of this book, something even I took as being quite trivial, was the resentment that Don had towards his professional life."

"She's lying!" Rhod cried out. "They both are!"

The journalist smiled at him. "Don Fletcher, a world-renowned psychic medium, was, in fact, a self-confessed performer. He didn't believe in ghosts or spirits anymore than I do. But he had spent his entire life putting on an act. He had fooled the world and reaped the rewards. Don Fletcher, the ghost whisperer, was merely a persona. And after a whole career of maintaining his illusion, he was finally ready to pull off the mask." She pointed to Rhod, who seemed on the verge of tears. "So you can imagine how it must have felt when your greatest hero asks to look over his final piece of work. It can't be easy finding out that your idol turns out to be a fraud."

Rhod leapt forward and tackled her to the floor. Alun followed after him, and with the help of a few volunteers, managed to drag the teenager away before he could dig his fingers into her throat.

"Is that the reaction you had when Don asked you to read his new book?" Rhiannon asked, still coughing from the attempted strangle. "The man was morphined up to the eyeballs that night. It wouldn't have taken much to add a little extra into his syringe. All you had to do was hold him under the water. Then, if you were really clever, there was still time to put his book right."

"You'll never understand what it's like!" Rhod screeched. "To have everyone calling you a freak! I've been blessed with a gift, and Don was about to make a mockery of everything I believe in! He was the only person who didn't make me feel alone — didn't make me feel strange. And then he was going to ruin everything!"

"I'm sorry to interrupt," said a curious Officer Gwent. "But how on earth do you arrive at a solution as bonkers as this? I mean, there was no more evidence in that room than we had."

"It all started with the plug hole," said Alun.

"Excuse me?"

"The plug." The accountant turned to face Rhod. "It was something you said to me when we were down at the harbour that first planted the seed, and a seed was all I needed, at first." He asked the policeman: "Which direction are your feet facing when you take a bath, Officer?"

Officer Gwent had to think about it. "Why, facing the taps, of course."

Alun pointed to a random member of the crowd. "And you?"

"I take showers," said the concierge. "But I suppose, if I *did* take a bath, yeah, my feet would be pointing to the taps."

"As I believe most people would," said Alun. "But unlike

most people, Don took baths with his *back* facing the taps. That means he was literally sitting on the plug. Very unusual." He turned back to Rhod. "Which is why it struck me as very odd that this young man mentioned to me that he wished his idol could have *reached straight down* and pulled out the plug at the very last second. How did he know the direction Don was lying to be able to do that — if he was never even there that night?"

Both the police officer and the detective were quite flummoxed.

"That was it?" asked DCI Neale. "That little vague comment was enough?"

Alun nodded at him. "You of all people should know, detective, that it only takes a tiny spark to get your mind thinking." The man shook his head in disgust. "Then there was the big storm. Rhod told us he was at home watching the new episode of *Doctor Who* around the time of Don's death. But I later found out that the entire village lost its power that night."

"Once that seed is planted," Rhiannon added, "the growing never stops."

Her friend nodded.

"So are you telling us Gwen knew it was him the whole time?" Mared asked. "Why didn't she tell anyone?"

"Because she had her own secret to keep," replied Rhiannon. "Unfortunately, Rhod knew that Gwen had seen him. And what followed was another murder attempt."

"Another one?!" Rowena Tudor asked in horror.

"The first time he tried locking her in the sauna," said Alun.

"That was just to scare her off," Rhod grumbled. "I never wanted to kill her."

"But she did want to kill you, didn't she?" Rhiannon asked him. "That night at the party."

"She messaged me to come up to her room," the teenager

said, his rage now having mellowed into self-pity. "When I got there she was still drunk and holding a hammer. She said I couldn't scare her anymore, and threatened to bash my face in right then and there. But she couldn't do it. So I left."

Alun nodded. "So now we're left with a hammer by the bed and a sleeping partner who is known to have violent outbursts when he gets bad dreams."

Now it was Rhiannon's turn to nod. "Not the best combo for a quiet night's sleep. It never boded well for her."

Tears erupted from the victim's distraught mother.

"So Johnny *did* murder Gwen?" asked the excited concierge. "And he doesn't even remember it?"

"So it would seem," said Alun. "Unless the man really *did* want to get caught."

"Or was very stupid," Rhiannon added.

There was a lot of whispering going on now among the hotel staff. This was an afternoon they would be talking about for a very long time. But one person who was not doing any further talking was Rhod, and Rhiannon felt it was time to set one last thing straight.

"Can I ask you something, Rhod?" The teenager looked up. "Why on earth did you think it was a good idea to invite me up here?"

"Because people believe what you write. Like that story about the witch. I wanted your coverage of this story to go viral. I wanted everyone to know that my gift is real. That Don was real. That people like me aren't crazy."

"Not crazy?!" Angela Pugh shouted. "I think if there's one thing you've failed miserably at, young man, it's proving you're not crazy!"

Alun watched the teenager hang his head. For a split second, despite everything Rhod had done, he still felt a degree of pity for him. Then he remembered about the bath. Perhaps he would stick with taking showers from now on.

Through the crowd of onlookers, he thought he had seen a vision of his father's face peering back at him. Whether it had been a ghost or a figment of his imagination, the expression on the man's face was very clear: he had been very proud.

CHAPTER 30

The final breakfast at the *Balamon Hotel* had been as unexciting as it had been every morning. On this morning, however, it tasted better than anything Alun had eaten in quite some time. Perhaps it was not the ingredients that were responsible, but the fact that they were about to embark on their journey back to Pengower.

The case of Don Fletcher and his untimely death was now closed. These two visitors from Merioneth had done their bit with assisting the local police force, and it was looking likely that the graves of Tremor were going to be dug by someone other than the Roberts brothers from now on.

Rhiannon was also over the moon, as she had amassed more than enough content for her next article, and her editor-in-chief was looking forward to reading about a haunted hotel, where the living were far more dangerous than the dead.

As the two companions made their way back across the Menai Bridge, Alun bid a last, private farewell to the island that would now hold a lot of memories (some of them good, some of them bad and most of them very strange).

The Lighthouse Family's greatest hits were filling the car

with an upbeat mood. As the accountant listened to the opening verse of the song "High", he thought about how much he was going to miss his friend's company. He knew that the reality of their normal day-to-day lives back in Pengower was going to be very different to that of their trip. Their time together was not going to be nearly as frequent, and that idea filled him with a great sadness.

Perhaps it really was time for him to tell Rhiannon how he really felt. The woman's brief flirtation with Johnny Roberts had taught him that time was growing short, and if he didn't make a move soon, then another person undoubtedly would.

Listening to his driver singing out the words of a nineties pop classic, he decided that he would place his heart on the line as soon as they were back in Pengower. Perhaps she would feel the same as he did, or perhaps she wouldn't. For the time being, Alun was perfectly happy to enjoy the moment, and, with a carefree attitude that was quite uncharacteristic of him, he reached for the car radio and cranked the volume right up.

ABOUT THE AUTHOR

We hope you enjoyed this book. If you'd like to read more books in this new series, you can join the P. L. Handley e-mail newsletter and receive all the latest news on future releases.

Subscribe to the e-mailing list by visiting the official P. L. Handley website at: www.plhandley.com

Reviews are extremely important for new authors, so please feel free to leave a short review on the book's Amazon page. Doing so will be a huge support in helping to introduce other new readers to this book.

Stay tuned for Book Three in the Murder Ledger Mysteries:

Final Score

Coming Soon...

Printed in Great Britain
by Amazon